Levity glimmered in Charity's eyes. Rick was tempted to tell his best knock-knock joke just to see her laugh again.

But he waited too long, and she started moving closer to the church entry, away from him.

She glanced at her watch. "I need to grab this…stuff and get home," she said. "I have to work tonight." With a wave, she turned and pulled open one of the double-glass doors.

Rick waved back, wishing he could think of an excuse to stall her. The way she blurred the clear lines around his personal boundaries, he should have been wishing she would disappear until the building dedication instead of hanging around and distracting him.

Climbing back on the ladder, he still couldn't help observing when her car pulled out of the church lot. And more than that, he couldn't help wondering when he'd see her next. Or hoping it wasn't too long.

Books by Dana Corbit

Love Inspired

A Blessed Life #188
An Honest Life #233

DANA CORBIT

has been fascinated with words since third grade, when she began stringing together stanzas of rhyme. That interest, and an inherent curiosity, led her to a career as a newspaper reporter and editor. After earning state and national recognition in journalism, she traded her career for stay-at-home motherhood.

But the need for creative expression followed her home and, later, through the move from Indiana to Milford, Michigan. Outside the office, Dana discovered the joy of writing fiction. In stolen hours, during naps and between carpooling and church activities, she escapes into her private world, telling stories from her heart.

Dana makes her home in Grand Rapids, Michigan, with her husband, three young daughters and two cats.

AN HONEST LIFE

DANA CORBIT

Published by Steeple Hill Books™

STEEPLE HILL BOOKS

Steeple
Hill™

ISBN 0-373-87243-7

AN HONEST LIFE

Copyright © 2003 by Dana Corbit Nussio

Visit us at www.steeplehill.com

Printed in U.S.A.

No man has ever seen God; if we love one another,
God abides in us and His love is perfected in us.

—I John 4:12

To my grandmother, Jane Bowley,
who shares my love of romance and whose own
story of lifetime love inspires me.

A special thanks to the following people
for lending your expertise to this story:
Angela Jacobson, R.N., labor and delivery nurse;
Lisa Cardle, R.N., neonatal intensive care nurse;
Dr. Steven Naum, M.D., hand surgeon;
and Duane Rasch and Jon Tuthill, licensed builders.
Any mistakes contained within are my own.

Chapter One

Adrenaline pumped through Charity's veins in the same rhythm that her soft-soled shoes tapped on the hallway floor. She rushed into her sixth labor-delivery-recovery-postpartum room since the seven-to-seven shift started five hours before. And for the sixth time, she grumbled about the barometric pressure changes that likely had triggered labor for so many women. Thanks to it, Stanton Birthing Center had become a madhouse over Labor Day weekend. And this was just barely Saturday morning.

Sucking in a breath of that familiar disinfectant scent, she knocked and pushed open the door. "Hello, Mr. and Mrs.—" she paused, gazing up from her chart to the woman on the bed and the man next to her "—Westin." She swallowed hard, her heart racing, her hands damp.

How could she have missed the connection when she'd read the name *Westin* on the room-status board?

Too late. Now she had to face these two people and the most humiliating moment of her life.

Andrew Westin coughed into his hand before he finally could say, "Hello, Charity." His wife said nothing at all, her eyes wide.

With a nod in his direction, Charity turned back to her patient. Serena Jacobs Westin chewed her lip, appearing pained, though the monitor attached to her belly showed she was between contractions. Charity could relate to that nonphysical agony.

"Mrs. Westin, I'll be your nurse throughout the night."

Throughout the night? Could she survive that long in the same room with the man she'd pined over and who had rejected her so soundly? Or with the former divorcée Andrew had chosen over her? Charity itched to run for the door, to take that much needed vacation far away from southeast lower Michigan, or at least to beg another labor and delivery nurse to take her patient. But she resigned herself to the task. Other staff members were already busy with two ongoing cesarean sections and a "mec" delivery—where an infant's waste, called meconium, was present in its amniotic fluid and signaled possible complications. She needed to buck up and do her job.

Wrapping the blood pressure cuff around Serena's arm, she set up the stethoscope to check her heart rate. "I need to get your vital signs and ask you a few questions before the staff obstetrician examines you. The admitting clerk said your water broke. Can you tell me at what time?"

Serena glanced at Andrew and turned back to her nurse. "Okay. Wait…I'm starting another one." She gripped her rounded abdomen and focused on a spot on the opposite wall, making the quiet *hee-hee* sound of Lamaze breathing.

"Come on, sweetheart, breathe," Andrew crooned, holding his wife's hand and brushing dark hair back from her face. "That's right. You're doing great."

If a hole in the floor could have swallowed her, Charity would have welcomed its suction. Instead, she fussed with the thick band that held her hair away from her face. Watching the loving way Andrew ministered to Serena only reminded Charity of what she didn't have. But she couldn't think about that now. Nor would she acknowledge the sharp edge of envy that pressed against her insides.

"He's right, Mrs. Westin. You're doing a great job, and your contraction has ended." Charity surprised herself by sounding in control, though her mind raced in a dozen directions. To maintain that illusion, she returned to her memorized list of questions. "About your water…"

"Nine o'clock," Serena answered, sounding strained.

That voice, more than her patient's response, focused Charity's thoughts immediately. It hinted that the baby might come soon. She bent to check the paper strip spilling from the fetal monitor. At least she saw no signs of early or late heart rate deceleration that might have indicated fetal distress.

"When is your due date?"

"September 8," she choked out.

Jotting down the gestation and other information the couple provided about Serena's last OB visit, Charity continued, "When is the last time you ate or drank anything?"

"Dinner…at six." Serena closed her eyes, another contraction coming on the heels of the former.

A knock came on the door just as Charity glanced at the monitor again, and a petite woman in blue scrubs stepped into the room.

"Hello, I'm Dr. Kristen Walker, the staff OB."

"Doctor, I'd like you to meet Andrew and Serena Westin."

Charity stepped next to the doctor, who was pulling on a pair of latex gloves. "Mrs. Westin is at thirty-nine weeks three days gestation. When she saw her OB two days ago, she was closed, thick and long. She ruptured at twenty-one hundred and could be precipitous. Her tones look good and her vitals are fine."

With Dr. Walker's nod, Charity moved to the wall telephone to contact Serena's regular obstetrician while the staff physician checked the degree of dilation and effacement.

Just as Charity hung up, Dr. Walker straightened and dropped her gloves into the garbage. "Mrs. Westin, you're already to eight centimeters and one hundred percent effaced. Your doctor is on her way. Keep up your Lamaze breathing because you'll be ready to push soon."

Charity moved into action, opening the cherry-finished cabinetry of the homey LDRP room, to reveal the necessary equipment for the delivery. In the infant care center, she turned on the warmer light, prepared the parent-newborn bracelets and readied the oxygen and suction equipment.

"Is she too far along for an epidural?" Andrew asked the doctor.

"I'm afraid so," Dr. Walker responded. "Everything will progress quickly now."

Their voices seemed so far away as Charity focused on her role in preparing for the big arrival. The baby hadn't even crowned and already she felt that same rush of excitement she experienced every day on the job. No matter how many newborns she cradled in her arms, the miraculous birthing process still amazed her.

But it wasn't time to be amazed yet. So much could still go wrong.

As soon as Dr. Walker left the room, Charity moved quickly to start Serena's IV. "We'll have to answer some of the standard questions after you deliver, but I already know the one about religion," she said as she secured the tube with medical tape.

Fifteen minutes later, Serena's regular obstetrician whipped through the door, yanking on his gloves. While the physician examined the mother and announced her ready to push, Charity checked to ensure they were prepared for the best…and the worst. Then she held her breath and braced one of her patient's legs while awaiting the miracle of life.

Charity wondered if she'd ever had a longer twelve-hour shift as she pulled her champagne-colored coupe out of West Oakland Regional Hospital's parking lot, practically letting her car drive itself back from Commerce Township to the Village of Milford. Her adrenaline boost had disappeared, leaving only her normal void.

A sad smile pulled at her lips when she thought of sweet Seth, who had announced his arrival with a howl that said, "Here I am." The Westin baby had chubby cheeks and blue eyes that were already threatening to turn brown. But like all the other newborns sleeping in the nursery or rooming with their mothers, he was someone else's child.

"Get over it, Charity," she said aloud, shaking her head at the empty road she traveled. Helping with Serena Westin's delivery had taken a heavier toll than she'd expected.

She hoped it was only her pulse—instead of her biological clock—that pounded in her ears. Whatever it was, it refused to let her favorite contemporary Christian music in the cassette player drown it out. December and her thirtieth birthday loomed before her, and she didn't have a marriage prospect in sight.

Figuring she wouldn't get any sleep this morning anyway, she continued up General Motors Road instead of turning on South Milford Road and heading straight home. Mother wouldn't mind. She wouldn't be up for breakfast for another hour anyway.

At Hickory Ridge Road, Charity turned right. A few miles up on the left, Hickory Ridge Community Church's well-tended flower beds—her work, of course—promised the gardening therapy and solace she needed. Focusing her thoughts on the gardening gloves, trowel and pruning shears she always kept in the trunk, she flicked back a seed of misgiving. Church hadn't offered her much peace lately, often unsettling her nerves. Even at her weekly prayer meetings, she'd felt empty. That wouldn't happen this time, when she could soak up the silence in the late summer sunshine—alone.

But as soon as she turned into the church drive, she realized how wrong she was. The whir of power saws and the bam-bam-bam of hydraulic nail guns reverberated off the windshield and filtered in the open window, setting her teeth on edge. *Can nothing go right today?*

R and J Construction had been working several weeks on the new Family Life Center building project, but she wished they'd taken this particular Saturday off. She drove farther until she reached the new asphalt parking lot past the parsonage. As soon as she shut off the engine, blaring rock music from the building site assailed her ears and had her grinding her molars.

Ignore it. She retrieved her gardening equipment and headed over to the farthest point away from that skeleton of a building—the landscaped bed on the side of the church facing the road. But tuning out those worldly sounds proved impossible, even as she dug below the roots of a grass clump that had dared invade the mulch-covered area.

"That's enough," she announced, just as a second song started beating its way into her mind.

Righteous indignation straightened her posture as she marched toward the construction site and a man dressed in faded jeans and a white T-shirt. As he straightened from bending over two sawhorses, she recognized him. He'd been at the center's ground-breaking ceremony.

"Excuse me," she said in her loudest speaking voice, suddenly uncomfortable to still be wearing her blue hospital scrubs out in public.

He jerked his head up. "May I help you?" he called out, shoving light brown hair out of his eyes.

"If you don't mind..." She crossed her arms and let her words trail off, figuring them useless under the power saw's drone and that incessant drumbeat.

The man pointed to his ears and shook his head. "Sorry. Can't hear you."

Charity didn't like the way his cornflower-blue eyes twinkled or the way his mouth turned up slightly at the corners. This was not funny. Stepping closer, she yelled again. "You might be able to if we didn't have to shout over that...noise."

The man turned his head to the right and executed a piercing two-finger whistle. Church member Rusty Williams appeared from the other end of the framed structure and, at his boss's nod, turned off the stereo. Amazingly, the saw stopped at the same time.

"Good to see you, Sister Charity," Rusty said, pausing beside them. "Did you just get off work? I didn't realize you two had met."

Charity nodded at the question and forcibly dropped her hands to her sides, trying not to smile at Rusty's habit of calling church members "brother" or "sister." Hardly anyone else at church—especially anyone as young as Rusty—referred to other members that way. Finally, she responded to his second comment. "We haven't really."

Rusty grinned and stood between them. "Charity Sims, I'd like you to meet R.J.—I mean Rick McKinley, owner of R and J Construction, the general contractor on the project." He turned to his boss. "Rick, I'd like you to meet Sister Charity, another fine member of Hickory Ridge Church. Now if you two will excuse me…" He started to walk away but turned back. "Oh, tell your mother hello for me, okay?"

Nodding, she turned back to Rick. He shoved his hair out of his eyes again. In need of a good cut, his hair was sun streaked from outdoor work.

"Now, you were saying…" he prompted, interrupting her observation.

"I was trying to say you could help me by turning off that awful music."

He shrugged, that infuriating grin returning, as he indicated with his head toward the boom box that was indeed already turned off. "So?" he challenged.

Charity stiffened again, the power of her conviction making it impossible to relax. "You must know that music like that is inappropriate for work at a church setting."

He nodded slowly, tucking thumbs through his tool

belt in a casual pose, but his chiseled jaw tensed. "I'm sorry you feel that way, Miss Sims, but music makes work easier for my crew. Especially on a holiday weekend when every other Michigander is fishing at a cabin up north or cruising the big lake."

Her arms folded again over her chest. How obtuse could this man be? "Mr. McKinley, it's not music I'm opposed to. It's the type you chose. Secular? Here at our church? What would people think if they drove up to meet with Reverend Bob Woods, our youth minister Andrew Westin or the deacons?"

His gaze hardened, and he seemed to have tightened all over. Sturdy muscles in his arms strained against his shirt. "They'd probably think my construction crew was playing some music. It's not even offensive music. Just run-of-the-mill pop."

"Whatever it is—" she paused, nodding toward the despised radio "—it doesn't belong here at Hickory Ridge. I can't believe you would defend it after I've made that clear to you."

"Oh, you've made something clear, all right." He jutted his chin forward. "You've proved a point, but it has nothing to do with music."

Charity gritted her teeth, her face becoming hot. Why did she have to put up with this impossible man? "I have no idea what you're talking about, but I insist that you keep that music turned off."

He stared at her a few seconds, his gaze furious enough to make her step back if she weren't so determined to hold her ground. The mission of the righteous was never easy. When she was certain she couldn't stay in that position a second longer facing his challenging stare, he jerked his hand sharply and startled her.

That hand ended up in an exaggerated salute at Rick's forehead. "Yes, ma'am." With that, he stalked over to the boom box, flipped the power switch and cranked the volume full blast.

"I said turn it off," she shouted.

Rick glanced back at her and pointed to his ears, indicating he couldn't hear what she was saying. Her hands tightened at her sides as she marched toward him. Rick McKinley would get a piece of her mind if she had to jam it right into his smug face. But when she got close enough to do just that, he didn't even give her the satisfaction of meeting her gaze. Something behind her seemed to have all of his attention.

Unable to resist seeing what was more important than listening to her, she glanced over her shoulder. Andrew Westin's car pulled farther up the drive, past the aging farmhouse that served as a parsonage, right toward them.

Her anger evaporated as embarrassment covered her like a sunbath. Charity shot a glance back at Rick before she turned to watch Andrew park and climb out of his car.

Why did she continually make a fool of herself in front of men? Why had she blown her top over something as trivial as a radio station? Antagonism from an infuriating man wasn't excuse enough. No matter what her reasons for rebuking the builder—or for that other unpleasant showdown in her past—she didn't plan to wait around to face both of these guys together.

"Obviously, I'm not going to get through to you, so I'm leaving," she shouted, hiding behind a facade of anger. With that, she about-faced and stalked to the parking lot, passing Andrew without a wave. She wished she didn't wonder about the looks focused on her back or why nothing made sense anymore.

Chased by feelings that had everything—and nothing—to do with the two men behind her, she rushed to the car and her escape. Only after she'd shot up some gravel in the church drive and had reached Hickory Ridge Road could she finally let go of the breath she'd held. Her relief was short-lived, though, as it was followed by hot and humiliating tears.

Chapter Two

Andrew Westin's lips moved, but Rick couldn't hear a word over the blaring radio. Feeling sheepish for letting that self-righteous so-and-so push his hot button, Rick jogged over to the boom box and shut off the power. *Great, now you're going to lose the contract. What will you do next, spit at Reverend Bob?*

"Hey, Andrew, sorry about that."

But the youth minister only waved away the apology, his focus on Charity's retreating car. A smile lit his face when he finally turned back to Rick. "Did you hear me, man? It's a boy." It didn't seem to matter to Andrew that he looked like he hadn't slept since the Fourth of July and his hair had hat head, minus the hat.

"Oh, that's great." Rick stepped forward and gripped the other man's hand. "Congratulations." Andrew's laughter was so contagious that Rick couldn't help joining in, despite his sour mood.

"It all happened so fast. He's so tiny. It was exciting and scary. You just wouldn't believe—"

"Is the baby okay?" Rick interrupted, trying to decipher the cryptic dialogue. "Is your wife okay?"

Andrew beamed as he breathed deeply and started again. "He's great. Serena's great. Eight pounds, twelve ounces. Him, not her. A head full of dark hair. That's the both of them." He stopped to chuckle at his joke. "Seth Michael Westin. Our boy." He stepped away long enough to pass blue bubblegum cigars out to several crew members before handing one to Rick.

What did that kind of joy feel like? Rick couldn't begin to guess, and he refused to let himself wonder and risk wishing. "What good news," he said when he could think of nothing else to say.

Rusty saved him from further platitudes by hurrying through the framed area where they would eventually hang glass double doors. Never one to worry about his manly-man image, Rusty wrapped Andrew in a bear hug that had to hurt.

"Brother Andrew, don't tell me you got yourself a boy." He slapped the youth minister's back when he finally released him.

"Sure did." Andrew stuffed a plastic-wrapped gum cigar into the other man's mouth. "He's a keeper, too."

Rusty pulled the candy out of his mouth and twirled it in his fingers. "What does your sweet stepdaughter think of her baby brother?"

"Tessa hasn't met him yet. I'm going to shower

and then pick her up from Robert and Diana Lidstrom's, so we can go visit Mommy and Seth.''

''Did the delivery go okay?'' Rusty asked the question casually, leaning against the sawhorse in the relaxed pose of a seasoned father of three. ''Any complications?''

''No, it was real easy—at least for me.'' Andrew laughed again. ''But it was strange having Charity as the labor and delivery nurse.'' He glanced back to the drive Charity had just exited.

''Isn't she great?'' Rusty must have missed the way Rick tensed and Andrew startled when he said that. ''She was in there when Tricia had Max two years ago. Didn't even break a sweat when Max came breech and ended up in an emergency C-section.''

As the two sang more of Charity's praises, Rick stepped away from both the conversation and comments he couldn't reconcile with the scrubs-wearing shrew, who had made his acquaintance with a sledgehammer. At least he'd moved far enough away that they wouldn't expect him to comment when Andrew wondered aloud why the object of their discussion had just raced from the church lot.

''Probably some woman thing,'' one of them said, with the other buying that easy explanation.

Rick didn't believe there was anything *easy* about understanding what made Charity Sims tick—double time. But then why was he wasting precious seconds thinking about that irrational woman? Just who did she think she was, anyway, being the censor and church police, all rolled up into one?

Everything about her was ironic, her name most of all. Charity. He couldn't imagine anyone *less* charitable. And that sun-kissed exterior of hers couldn't have been more incongruent with the dark inside he'd glimpsed. Without invitation, long tresses of golden thread appeared in his thoughts. She'd worn her hair tied back, but a few strands had escaped, making him imagine a riotous mane had it all been set free. But the green-gold eyes he envisioned next, their superior expression judging and convicting him with a single glance, cleared his thoughts of such nonsense.

This woman was a perfect example of why he kept his personal relationship with God just that—personal. She reminded him of those biblical Pharisees, praying out loud on the temple steps for show while they didn't know the Father at all deep inside, where it counted. Was she just like them, a hypocrite play-acting her faith for an audience? She'd certainly deserved applause for that performance on the church lawn.

"Boss, if you're planning to daydream all morning, then the rest of us would like to head off on our Labor Day weekend."

Rusty's chiding sent Rick slamming back to earth, bringing resentment along for the ride. "Funny, I thought my foreman and crew didn't have to be led by the hand." The words were barely out of his mouth, and he already regretted them. Rusty Williams was his best friend—his only friend. He'd never let anyone else get that close. "Hey, sorry—"

But the foreman shook it away with a wave and

grin. Good ol' Rusty. Rick moved back to his power saw as the table saw across the building site roared to life. As he marked a two-by-four to be cut, he concluded he wouldn't waste any more energy thinking about the motivations of the annoying Charity Sims.

He would focus on more important things like completing this center project on time and proving that R and J Construction was ready to add more commercial projects to its residential work. Instead of worrying about that woman's contradictions, he would concentrate on the irony that the Hickory Ridge project presented. In order to push his company firmly out of the red column and into the black, he had to work in the one place he had long disdained—a church.

Charity parked in the garage but couldn't convince her body to climb out of the car. That made no sense at all. She needed to get her thoughts in perspective, and who better to help her than Mother? Laura Sims would applaud her, first for her dignity in facing the Westin issue and later for her fortitude in putting that nasty general contractor in his place.

Why did that certain approval hold so little appeal for her today? Again, she wondered whether she'd been right to reproach the builder in front of his crew, even if he had been wrong. She still could see the shocked expression on his bronzed face and the contempt that had trailed so closely behind it. Could she possibly deserve his derision?

The squeak of the interior garage door helped her shake the image that filled her with humiliation rather than the holy vindication she would have expected.

"Charity, dear, you're not planning to spend the whole morning in the car, are you?" Laura stood in the doorway, wiping her hands on her apron. "I've been holding breakfast for you, and here you are letting it get cold while you sit behind your steering wheel."

"Sorry, Mother—"

"I should think so. I didn't even get a call that you would be late. I deserve that much consideration. You know how I worry."

As much as she resented her mother playing her, Charity felt her strings being plucked and recognized she had no choice but to produce a melody. "I don't know what I was thinking. I should have called, but I didn't want to wake you. I know how you like to sleep in on Saturdays."

She would have mentioned she was twenty-nine years old—plenty old enough to care for herself—if she'd thought it would have made a difference. It wouldn't have.

"But it's even more important to me to know you're safe," Laura responded as she pulled her daughter into the house. "You're all I have since your father went to his heavenly home, bless his sweet soul."

Hearing the standard soliloquy on her late father's many attributes cuing up, Charity spoke quickly to interrupt the tape. "I'm glad you care, Mother. Now let's eat before your great breakfast gets cold."

Between bites of eggs and fried potatoes, Charity filled her mother in on the details of her embarrassing experience at the hospital. She mentioned stopping by the church as an aside.

"Oh, you poor dear." Laura made a tsk-tsk sound and shook her head before sipping her coffee. "That had to have been so difficult. We both thought Andrew was the perfect choice for you—the Lord's choice. He *seemed* so much like your dear father. But Andrew's decision to marry *that divorcée* shows we were mistaken."

Obviously. And apparently Laura still resented the woman who'd eliminated her daughter's chance at the handsome youth minister. She wished her mother would just let it go, as Charity finally had. Especially after today.

"I'm fine, Mother."

"Sweetheart, the godly man we've always hoped for is out there somewhere, waiting for you. We have only to wait for God to reveal His plan."

"I know you're right," she answered, anything but sure. How many times had she heard those same words—and believed them? So why did they sound so empty now?

Absently tracing patterns in her remaining scrambled eggs, Charity let the questions plaguing her lately resurface. She'd always figured with her devout mother and near-sainted late father, she'd received faith as a birthright. The rest she was beginning to question. But what more could she do? She already walked the Christian walk and talked its talk head and shoulders better than others in her church. Not that she expected a reward, but didn't God answer the prayers of the faithful?

As if she noticed how quiet Charity had become, Laura reached over and squeezed her hand. "I'm just sure you'll meet him soon."

Charity's fork stilled as Rick's face—too handsome for his own good—sneaked uninvited into her thoughts. She'd met a "him" all right, but if first impressions could be trusted, he didn't belong in this conversation at all.

"Good, you can be sure for the both of us." If only her attempt at humor didn't sound so strained.

"What did you work on at the church?" Laura asked as she cleared away the dishes.

"I couldn't get focused. I didn't get much done." She couldn't explain why she was reluctant to discuss that exchange with Rick, even if her mother had given her a perfect opportunity to broach the subject.

Laura offered her a closed-lipped, all-knowing mother smile. "You probably just got impatient and left. You've always been impatient."

The comment ruffled her, but Laura was right. If not for Charity's rush to find a husband, maybe she wouldn't have chased Andrew so desperately or been so furious when he rejected her. Not for the first time, she wondered if her accusing him of having an affair with Serena had been inspired more by revenge than holiness.

She would have thought she'd learned a thing or two from that humiliating sequence of events. Like, for instance, that making rash judgments could result in undue embarrassment for all those involved. Andrew had told her there was a perfectly good explanation for his overnight presence at Serena's house, if she would only wait for it. But Charity hadn't waited; she'd gone right to the deacons with her charge. And then it had come to light how Andrew and Serena had been counseling Reverend Bob's pregnant teenage daughter.

Shame over that situation still made Charity hang her head low. *If you learned so much, what were you doing, attacking that poor builder?* That Rick McKinley was wrong suddenly didn't seem a good enough defense for her actions.

"Charity, dear, stop daydreaming and eat some toast. You're going to waste away to nothing. And just look at your eyes. You look exhausted."

Maybe that's because I worked all night. That unkind response startled Charity so much she straightened in her chair. Guilt appeared immediately, but she covered it with a smile and a nod. It wasn't like her to talk back to her mother, even in her thoughts. Mother always had her best interest at heart. She needed to remember that. "You're right. I am tired."

"You go straight to bed then. I'll clean up the kitchen. I did most of the cleaning while I was waiting for you, anyway."

"Thanks, Mother," she said, choosing not to respond to that last comment or the mild censure that came with it.

Charity let herself be shooed up the stairs to her room, but the tiny daisies that covered the bed, walls, filmy curtains, even her picture frames, immediately crowded her. It was a little girl's room. Nothing had changed in that room in twenty years, except the grade level of shelved textbooks and the arrival and upgrades in her desktop computer.

She couldn't sleep here, or anywhere else. Not as confused as she felt after the events at the hospital. And not with Rick McKinley's smug face reappearing in her thoughts. Before this morning, she'd only seen him that one time at the groundbreaking, and now his image wouldn't go away. More frustrating than that, just one confrontation with this guy had dissatisfaction with her whole life twisting inside her like a tightening noose.

That made no sense. Her life was fine. Settled, even. So it had to be something else. Something about the man himself. Crawling under her blankets, she tried to push away the images as well as the agitation that kept her breathing from steadying toward sleep. She could still see him measuring and sawing wood, outside in the September morning. Outside the church.

''Wait. That's it.'' She looked about the room, as surprised at having spoken aloud as having sat straight up in bed.

She'd never seen Rick *inside* her church. Maybe he didn't attend anywhere. Come to think of it, she didn't recognize any of the crew from Sunday services, and since she never missed one, she should know. Oh, Rusty attended regularly, of course, but the rest were definite prospects. Maybe her preoccupation with Rick was a sign of her mission to bring that motley construction crew into the church.

Letting her head float back to the pillow, she imagined all the men, tool belts still slung on their hips, lining the church's front pew. But her plan stalled, only halfway formed. Before she could act as a candle leading those men to light, she needed to make amends with their difficult leader.

A case of nerves. Nothing else could explain the way her pulse tripped at the thought of facing Rick again. She flipped onto her stomach, burying her face in the pillow and pressing her heart into the mattress to slow the beat.

Maybe it was anticipation for the mission ahead. It had nothing to do with being under the scrutiny of those huge, unreadable eyes or absorbing the tension he radiated in waves. No, she had been and would continue to be unaffected by the rugged Rick McKinley. But an uneasiness settling deep inside made her wonder.

Rick took the last bite of his sandwich during his lunch break, wishing he could bite back the resentment that had soured his mood all morning. That he couldn't shake the irritation only made him angrier. He stood up from the picnic table, stowed his cooler under a tree and stalked toward the building site.

Rusty caught up with him halfway across the parking lot and fell into step beside him.

"Hey, Boss, sorry about the run-in with Sister Charity. You've just got to understand that—"

"That what?" Rick jerked to a stop and faced the other man. "That she's a shrew? That she had nothing better to do than to come here and bother me?" He glanced at his shoulders that had lifted to about ear level and carefully lowered them to a relaxed pose. "No big deal."

Rusty nodded. "I can see that."

"Can see what?"

Rusty countered Rick's sharp look with a sheepish grin. "I know Sister Charity can get under the fingernails of the best of them, but she's not so bad really. She's got a real good heart when she lets it shine through. If I had my guess, I'd say it was her mother who taught her to hide it so well."

Rick didn't need to hear this, didn't care what made the spitfire spit. It was like hearing a serial killer explain how he didn't get enough hugs as a child. So he had no idea what made him ask, "What do you mean?"

"After Mr. Sims died, Sister Laura moved to Milford with Charity, who was about three from what I've heard tell. Her mother was a founding member of Hickory Ridge, around since the church still met in an empty storefront at Main and Commerce."

When Rick prompted him to move along in the story with a twirl of an index finger, Rusty held up his hand. "I'm getting there. It's said that the late

Joseph Sims was a real good Christian man, a deacon who had just been called into the ministry when he passed. Sister Laura has spent almost three decades preparing her daughter to marry someone just like him.''

Rick started walking again but turned to speak over his shoulder. "What does that have to do with attacking strangers on construction sites?"

Rusty raised both hands in a gesture of simplicity. "Charity is trying to act the part of a perfect minister's wife, hoping that will help her catch a minister. But she's got it all wrong.''

"That's pretty obvious, but I don't see how any of this matters.''

"Hear me out, okay?" Glancing first at the parsonage, Rusty turned back to his boss. "Almost two years ago, when Andrew started his fellowship at Hickory Ridge, Charity chased after him like toilet paper stuck to a shoe, and she was appreciated about as much. It was a real blow to her when he married Serena instead.''

Andrew and Serena who had just had a child together? With Charity as their nurse? A seed of pity for the woman he'd immediately disliked threatened to sprout inside Rick, but he pushed it safely underground. "I bet that made it uncomfortable today at the hospital.''

"It might have been, but I just know Sister Charity did everything she could to make the delivery comfortable for Serena. Charity's a great nurse. You can just tell how much she cares about those babies—and their moms. That's how I know she has a good heart.''

Rick took a few more steps away. "She wasn't displaying any *good heart* when she marched in and attacked me over my choice of music."

Rusty walked up behind him again. "Our Charity. What a gal." He laid a hand on his boss's shoulder until Rick faced him, and then Rusty leaned in for a close examination. "Well, it doesn't look like she left any marks—visible ones, anyway. Why don't you give her a break this time?"

"Yeah, you're probably right."

"Besides, it's not like you have to work with her every day or anything. You probably won't have to see her again until the dedication."

From your mouth to God's ears. But to Rick, he only said, "Okay. You're right." It was awfully hard for him to see gray in his black-and-white world, and his friend expected him to see the full range of hues from soft silver to dark steel. "But that woman is as pious as the rest of those church people I remember."

"I'm one of those *church people,* R.J., and you know me, warts and all. It's not fair to pile us into one pot any more than it would be for me to judge your relationship with God."

Rick stared at Rusty. He did know him, through years of work and through a friendship where the roots had grown deep. "Point taken. But hey, she attacked *me.*"

"I'm not debating that. I don't know what put a bee in her bonnet. But I'm telling you there's another side to Charity. The side that appears when she puts on her scrubs and heads into those fancy labor rooms.''

''Obviously, her transformation didn't work today because she had scrubs on when she was here.'' Rick tried a bit of humor, but Rusty shook his head, apparently not buying it.

''I'll never forget when she helped deliver Max.'' Rusty paused as if he was reliving that special day. ''When she handed me that big round boy, I saw tears in her eyes.''

Rick raised his hands in surrender. ''Okay, she's not completely evil.''

''Far from it, my friend.'' Rusty grinned and, without another word, turned and jogged to the rear of the building site that would eventually be the gymnasium.

Rick exhaled as he watched him, all of the wind ripped from his perfectly good rant. Watching the other workers, he had the creepy sensation that they'd been observing him during the discussion with Rusty. At least they couldn't have heard it. But the breath he exhaled, he immediately drew back in. Just how long had they stood there discussing this woman who was a stranger to him? Stranger? After that discussion, he knew more about Charity Sims' personal life than he'd learned about many crew members who had worked for him for months. Years even.

Rick tightened his tool belt and returned to the saw, hoping the blare would drown out thoughts of anything other than roofing trusses and subcontractors. Nothing would be allowed to divert his focus from completing this project on time and with the highest quality workmanship.

Sweaty work had always been his ticket out of his past and into the security and respect he craved. With this project, he could finally prove to those who believed he would amount to nothing that they were wrong.

Because it didn't make much difference when compared to such critical matters, he would cut Charity some slack. She would likely keep her distance from him now, anyway. If she didn't, well, he'd cross that bridge when he slammed into it.

Chapter Three

Two days later, Labor Day offered a sunny Monday off for many laborers, but fidgetiness kept Charity from enjoying the respite. Concentrating on the pots of chrysanthemums and garden tools at her feet was impossible when she only had to peek around the church building's corner to see the prospect who had become "priority one" in her mission work. Even on the holiday, Rick remained the lone construction worker, toiling as if some supervisor still had him on the clock. Or as if he had something to prove.

After adding another look in that direction to the dozen earlier, she regretted turning down her mother's invitation for their annual holiday outlet shopping spree. At the time, relaxation had seemed more important. Well, if relaxation wore grass-stained gardening shoes and was on constant alert, then she was well on the road to tranquility.

She continued yanking fists of dying wax begonias

from the earth, the loose dirt seeming the most solid thing beneath her lately. But finally she gave in to her curiosity and took another peek at the building project. Too bad Rick, sporting a Detroit Red Wings cap and sunglasses, picked that moment to trudge toward the front of the church building where she'd been working.

"Sure is a beautiful morning. It was, anyway." He stopped several feet away but gazed directly at her, sunlight catching on his unusual blue eyes. "It's afternoon now."

Though Charity's cheeks burned, and her mouth competed with the Sahara on the dryness scale, she managed an affirmative noise in her throat. An awkward silence followed until they both spoke at once to break it.

"Hey, I'm sorry—"

"You know, I'm sorry—"

Charity couldn't help laughing and felt relieved when Rick joined in. As he took a few more steps toward her, she scrambled to her feet. The filth she wiped from her palms to her holey jeans probably came with a dose of perspiration. She resisted the temptation to pat her hands on her loose ponytail. It shouldn't have mattered how she looked. "I wasn't bothering you, was I?"

"No. Was my noise bothering you? I didn't have any music on this morning." His smile was no less than devastating, that soft-looking mouth incongruous with the hard lines of his cheekbones. A small split tamed the perfection of his straight teeth.

Could her face and neck have gotten any warmer? "Uh…no. Of course not."

"I really am sorry about the other day. I was obnoxious."

How tempted she felt to let him take the blame for the whole crazy incident, but she resisted. She took her mission to bring this man to church seriously. To that end, she forced herself to look directly at him and to smile back. The Lord's work required great sacrifice.

"No, I'm the one who overreacted and berated you about the music," she said. "I went about it all wrong."

Stuffing his hands in his pockets as if suddenly more uncomfortable in the situation, Rick pressed his lips into a straight line. That only made more obvious how little about Rick McKinley was soft. Not his features, all sharp angles and hard planes, and not his physique, which appeared as hard as the bricks stacked next to the building.

At her realization she'd been gawking, Charity glanced away from him, ashamed. "I'd better get these planted."

She sat cross-legged on the ground, digging her fingers back into the earth. To safety. She pulled a few weeds, expecting him to retreat to the construction site. But he stayed there, staring across the field at Andrew and Serena's house.

"I didn't expect to see anyone here today," he said as he dropped to his knees a few feet from her and yanked out a handful of weeds. "I figured everyone would be grabbing that last taste of summer. All of my crew are doing that.''

''But not you.'' The words slipped past her better judgment before she could censor them. Her slip and his closeness made her so nervous she dropped the trowel and had to scramble to retrieve it. Now he probably thought she was wondering why he'd come here today and why he remained so close she could smell the sawdust on his clothes. And he would have thought right. ''Me, neither,'' she added in a rush. ''I'm ready for summer to be over. I thought I'd get a head start on fall while everyone else was gone.''

''Do you do all of the gardening work at the church?''

She almost smiled at that. And it pleased her more than it should have that he'd attempted to make conversation when he easily could have left. He probably just wanted someone to talk to, and his crew was off for the day. It wasn't as if he was interested in her or anything. They had nothing in common, as far as she could tell. Besides, she would never date a guy who quite possibly didn't even go to church.

''The trustees take care of the grounds, but I'm in charge of the landscape committee. I do what I can with a limited budget and donate the rest.''

He nodded and yanked off his cap, tucking it in the waistband of his pants. Though his hair was sweaty and mussed, Charity could tell he'd gotten a haircut and appeared almost presentable. He resumed plucking weeds, even reaching beside her to borrow the trowel and dig out a few deep roots.

"You do a good job," he said after a while.

It was the smallest of compliments, and yet Charity felt her insides warm with pleasure. From the way she'd reacted, she would have sworn he'd just dubbed her a master landscaper or something. "It looks bad right now."

"No, it looks in transition."

Neither said anything for a while, but they continued in companionable silence until they'd cleared the planting bed. "I have to get more plants from over there in the shade," she told him. He surprised her by following and helping her carry flowers.

"Thanks, but you don't need to do that. You'll probably want to get back to your own work."

Why had she encouraged him to leave when it was the last thing she wanted? But his nearness felt a little too nice to be a good idea.

"I don't mind." He laid the green plastic pots on the ground. "I needed a real break, anyway."

Charity turned her head away to hide her grin. In her defense, it had been an awfully long time since she'd had an actual conversation with someone who wasn't her mother, a co-worker or a fellow church member. But this wasn't about her. This conversation presented an opportunity, and she needed to get busy with church work.

"How is the project coming along?" she asked.

"Now that we've framed the walls, we'll be setting the trusses and sheathing the roof." He glanced back at the structure and shook his head. "Until the building has a roof, we can't install windows, doors or flooring.''

''Do you think you'll meet the November deadline?''

He shrugged. ''It's going to be tight. If all the subcontractors—plumbing, electric, heating and cooling, insulation, drywall and finish flooring—are on time, and that's a big if, then we've got a chance, anyway.''

''Oh, I hope everything moves quickly. That would be great if it would be ready for the Thanksgiving celebration.''

She dug a few holes and indicated for Rick to hand her individual plants to put into them. Once she lowered them into the ground and patted the dirt back into place, she turned back to him. ''Have you heard about that event? It's like a family holiday dinner times fifty.''

''Sounds okay, I guess, if you like things like that. But if anything throws the schedule off, it won't be happening this year inside the new building.''

''If the project is done, you'll come to the church celebration, won't you?''

He made a noncommittal sound and handed her another plant. Well, at least it wasn't an outright no. She could almost guarantee he'd be a regular church attendee before that next holiday.

She looked back at him again. ''How was your Labor Day weekend?''

''Short. I worked Saturday, remember? And isn't today still part of the long weekend?''

She nodded and took a deep breath before diving in. "Didn't see you at church Sunday."

"I wasn't there. I don't attend church."

Now that sounded like a definite no. Her confidence slipped, but it wasn't like her to give up easily. "You need to give it a chance, Rick. You'd just love Hickory Ridge. It's a great church community." She refused to hear how empty those words sounded in her ears or to wonder whether she even believed what she'd said. If the church was so great, then why did she feel so lonely lately every time she entered its doors?

"It's not your specific church I'm opposed to. I disagree with organized religion overall."

Charity's mouth went dry. How could anyone believe such a thing when church was so much a part of her life, the center point of her daily schedule? But then the shock evaporated into irritation. "If you don't believe in churches, then why are you building the Family Life Center?"

"I believe in honest work and giving clients the very best. And my foreman, Rusty, convinced me this was a good project for us—a group *he* believes in—so we went for the contract."

The dispassionate way he said it bothered her even more. "I don't understand how you can think this important project is just work. And if it's just about earning a living, then why are you here alone today when you won't accomplish much?"

Instead of answering her question, he shrugged. Charity planted her hands on her hips, refusing to wonder why his apathetic attitude annoyed her so much. Of course, it was justified, and she hurriedly searched for a reason to tell him before he spoke again. But he beat her to it.

"Hey, great news about the youth minister's new baby. I heard you helped with the delivery."

A punch couldn't have knocked the wind out of her as effectively as that statement had. Uneasiness put an end to her annoyance. How much did Rick know about Andrew? Had Andrew told him the whole embarrassing story?

Her thoughts whirling off-kilter, she struggled for some appropriate response. She had to think of something to say before the awkward pause in their conversation expanded like a fault line during an earthquake. In a rush, she choked out, "Yes, Seth is a sweet baby. He is so perfect—such a wonderful gift from God."

"That's funny," he said. "I thought they were all supposed to be gifts from God—even the less-than-perfect ones."

Charity jerked up her head, but he only looked away. That wasn't what she'd meant to say. He'd just gotten her all flustered, and now she'd fallen in a trap of her own words. Why did it seem she couldn't string two coherent thoughts together when this man was around?

"That's not what I meant, and you know it," she said, crossing her arms over her chest, part for effect and part as self-protection from the way he muddled her thoughts. "I know perfectly well that all children are precious to God. In Matthew 19:14, Jesus even says, 'Let the children come to me, and do not hinder them; for to such belongs the kingdom of heaven.'"

She couldn't help feeling a little smug over that comeback. That would show him not to twist her words.

But Rick only shook his head, a strange smile appearing on his lips. "Yes, the Bible is an amazing book, the Book of Matthew in particular, where the Beatitudes are found. One of them says 'Blessed are the meek, for they shall inherit the earth.' *Meek* and *humble* mean the same thing, don't they?"

Charity felt color draining from her face. He'd as much as accused her of having no humility. She searched madly for some appropriate retort, something to put this arrogant fool in his place, but she finally ran out of steam. "Oh...just forget it. Did you have some real purpose here, or did you just come to bother me?"

Rick made a negative sound and didn't meet her gaze when he said, "I didn't know you'd be here."

"Then why are you here? Really?"

"I thought it would be quiet at the site with the holiday and all." He shrugged and took a few steps toward his black extended cab pickup. Over his shoulder he said, "I came to pray."

To pray? Charity still reeled from Rick's words, even as she watched him dump his tools in the truck and drive from the church lot. Part of her wanted to offer him good riddance, while the other part wished to pepper him with questions. It made no sense that he would have such a problem with churches and yet come to pray at the deserted church lot. Come to think of it, why was he praying at all if he didn't attend church? And how was he quoting Scripture if he didn't hear it every week in sermons?

Was it possible for him to have faith, even if he didn't teach Sunday school or sing in the choir or, at the very minimum, attend Sunday services regularly? She just didn't know.

And equally confusing was how he seemed so intent on twisting everything she said to make her look bad. It was as if he wanted to make some statement, but whatever it was, she wasn't getting it.

At least he hadn't pushed the issue of the Westin baby or any nastiness from her past regarding Andrew. Maybe he didn't know as much as she'd first suspected. The relief that pushed a heavy breath from her lungs surprised her. Why did it matter so much that a near stranger didn't know about her less than shining past?

Gardening having lost its appeal, Charity gathered up her tools and crossed to her car. She refused to acknowledge the voice inside that questioned her leaving right then, when the church grounds were finally empty and she could work alone.

She needed to get home and rest; that was it. The excuse was sure easier to swallow than that she was still bothered by that conversation with Rick. And not just the mini scriptural debate, either. She'd had plenty of those over the years, and she could hold her own against all but the best-trained biblical scholars. Far more troubling was how enjoyable she'd found chatting with Rick and planting with him side by side.

The image of his startling blue eyes, with character lines crinkling at the corners, stole into her thoughts. How light and sparkling those eyes appeared when Rick laughed. How anger darkened that color at least two shades. She knew. She'd seen—and probably inspired—both reactions.

Suppressing that image took more energy than should have been necessary, but she'd accomplished it by the time she'd closed the car's trunk. Obviously, she had to be a little friendly with him to accomplish her mission of bringing him to church, but she wasn't supposed to enjoy herself so much. She admonished herself to focus on her Christian duty rather than the handsome prospect as she climbed behind the wheel.

But that didn't stop her from jerking her head sharply toward the sound of gravel being shot up at the end of the long church drive. Her pulse slowed only when inside the cloud of dust, she saw Andrew's car instead of a pickup. *You just didn't want to argue with him again,* she told herself, trying hard to believe it.

Obviously on the return ride from the hospital, Serena sat next to her husband, and a plastic handle from an infant car seat protruded from the center back seat. As they passed, Andrew stopped and rolled down his car window. Charity pressed her foot to the brake and hit the automatic window button.

A head full of dark curls suddenly pressed up

against the back of Andrew's seat, Tessa's tiny hand waving madly through the crack between the door-frame and the headrest. "Hi, Miss Charity. We have a new baby brother."

Teaching the Tiny Tot Sunday school class did have its advantages, like getting to know sweet little kids like this one. "That's great, Tessa. I heard you're a big sister. Boy, that's an important job."

"It sure is," the kindergartner announced and sat back to fuss over the bundle in the car seat.

Andrew shook his head, his grin so big his cheeks had to ache. "Are you having a good holiday, Charity?"

"Not as good as yours, having your family home again." Charity leaned forward so she could see the youth minister's wife. "Welcome home, Serena. I bet you're glad to be back." It was surprising how much easier it was to have a friendly conversation with the other woman after having served as her nurse. Until now, they'd been polite but not overly friendly.

"I'm looking forward to having food with flavor in it. The hospital menu was pretty bland, but I guess you already know that," Serena said just as Seth started fussing from Tessa's overzealous attention. "Oh, I forgot the sleepless nights. Looking forward to those, too."

Charity laughed with her. Not that she wouldn't mind walking the floors a few hours with her own colicky newborn, but she refused to be envious today. It only exhausted her. "Let me know if you need anything," she said and found that she meant it.

With a few waves and an increasing volume of newborn wails, the Westins drove past to park near the old barn behind the house. Charity continued out of the drive, her thoughts still on the family climbing out of the small car.

The Westins had given her an idea. Sure, she needed to continue her mission to bring Rick to church, but she shouldn't focus her ministry so singularly. There were plenty of other needs in the church she could address as well. The Westins might appreciate some help in adapting to life with their new baby, and Tessa probably needed a little extra attention right now because of her changed status in the family.

That was it. If she was busy ministering to *several* church families, she would be much too preoccupied to let her thoughts focus on one brooding man. The plan seemed pretty good, but for some reason, it still didn't allow her to relax. In theory, it sounded perfect, but she worried it would fail woefully in practice.

Chapter Four

Rick stomped into his downtown Milford house, not even taking the time to wipe off his work boots as he usually did. A little dirt couldn't harm the badly scarred hardwood floors he'd recently uncovered, but it seemed counterproductive to his restoration project to make things any worse. Today, though, he just didn't care.

He didn't even take time to admire his handiwork on the newly refinished crown moldings and six-panel doors, glancing beyond their glossy mahogany to the rest of the nearly gutted structure. Everything was dark and drab—just the way he felt.

Why couldn't I just avoid her? Now that was the question of the day. He could probably spend another year trying to figure out the answer to it. But for whatever reason, the flower beds she tended—or the gardener herself—had diverted his interest from his own work until he finally had no choice but to talk to her.

It was bad enough that he'd started round two in their featherweight matchup by mentioning the Westin baby. But then he'd made it worse by throwing her an uppercut to the chin for that sanctimonious-sounding comment about the baby being a gift from God. Every child was, and she hadn't specifically singled that one out. But he'd been unable to resist the temptation to put her in her place, anyway.

In his defense, a flimsy one at best, she had all but called him a "heathen" for working on the church project when he didn't attend. He sure hadn't done much to convince her otherwise, he thought, as he kicked aside a sealed can of wood stain.

A real Christian should have been able to take the high road—to turn the other cheek, even—from her uninformed judgments. The thought halted him in kitchen doorway before he could step on the cracked, yellow linoleum. Just past the entry, Rick opened the junk drawer beneath the wall telephone and rustled through the mess until he connected with one of his most special possessions, an old Gideon's New Testament, its cover reattached with the handyman's solution to all problems: duct tape. If only he could move beyond just learning the Scriptures and begin to follow the lessons inside it.

Conviction settled deep in his heart before he could tuck the Bible back in the drawer. Sure, Charity seemed to use Scripture as a weapon to protect her from whatever she was afraid of, but hadn't he done the same thing? He was as guilty as she, playing her same judgmental game.

Father, I'm having some trouble with this one. I'm sorry I've behaved so badly, but this Charity just gets under my skin. Please forgive me and give me patience for dealing with all difficult people.

He paused long enough to open the refrigerator, pull out the fixings for a turkey with Swiss sandwich and set the armload on the tile countertop. "You know how sanctimonious she is," he prayed aloud this time as he made the sandwich. "You know her...." He let his words trail off as a realization struck him again. "But I get the feeling she doesn't know you." His prayer ended without an "amen" as they would be talking more throughout the day.

After downing the sandwich, Rick grabbed a sander and started smoothing the rough spots on the stripped hardwood. Focusing on the scrape of the sandpaper and the earthy scent of the fine wood dust, he hoped to extricate thoughts of Charity from his mind. But she only burrowed through his consciousness in layers not unlike those he uncovered in the old wood.

Her face flashed before him again—the perfect, porcelain features and huge, almost golden eyes that showed every emotion from flattery to fury. He liked the former a lot better, especially combined with that girlish blush. And her small rosebud mouth...it sure contrasted with her penchant for speaking out of turn.

When he saw her again—and he no longer held any illusions that he could avoid her for the duration of the project—he vowed to be nice to her. No matter how hard she made it. He would be a loving Christian example to her if it killed him, and if he needed to spend more time with her—say dinner—to make that point, then—

"Knock it off." His words bounced off the walls as he reached for his hammer and aimed for an errant nail, landing on his thumb instead. "Ow!"

Could he have been attracted to Charity Sims? No, it couldn't be that. But she did pull at him somehow. Maybe it was an emptiness he sensed beneath her religious armor. Or maybe he'd just imagined that to excuse some of his earlier behavior.

Anyway, even if he was interested in her, it wouldn't have made a difference. She looked down at him, at least for his beliefs. And if *that* didn't matter to him, it just proved he'd spent way too many months—make that years—without as much as a coffee date.

Were he to choose someone for a romantic relationship, she would be someone kind and pure-hearted like Rusty's Tricia. Although Rusty had been young when they'd wed and had only become a man during their marriage, Tricia had stood steady by his side. Envious? Not at all. He was more amazed, really. Rusty and Tricia were the only couple he knew who contradicted his theory that true love, at least the romantic kind, didn't exist.

Why was he allowing himself to think those thoughts, anyway? About anyone, let alone someone like Charity Sims. He'd been on his own as long as he could remember. He liked being alone. Except for his relationship with God and, much later, Rusty, he had avoided the complications of friendships. It had been for the best.

Needing people could be disastrous for a loner like him. It would only make him vulnerable—something he couldn't allow. He could never again let himself be that lost child of his memories. The only way to avoid that was to rely only on the person beneath his own skin. He'd never needed anyone, and he wasn't about to start now.

Early Tuesday afternoon Rick perched two extra two-by-fours on his shoulder and headed back to the framed building. A noise to his right caught his attention, and he turned to see a familiar car coming up the drive. He didn't have to look twice to recognize the driver, and he smiled against his will.

"Here we go again," he said, unloading his cargo onto the stack before glancing back at the parking lot.

If the idea of another verbal sparring round with Charity bothered him so much, then he shouldn't have been sauntering right to her, his heart tapping out Morse code in his chest. He reminded himself of a clown punching bag, the kind with sand in the bottom to keep it popping back up for more punishment.

But his comparison didn't stop him from stepping next to her car when she parked it and bending to speak into her open window. "We've got to stop meeting like this. People will talk."

Her hair wasn't tied back this time but flowed to her shoulder blades in a wavy mass. A crazy temptation to see if her tresses felt like silk had him tucking his thumbs safely through his tool belt.

Instead of saying something clever, she blushed. "I came to pick up some materials for my Sunday school class."

"Did you forget them when you were here yesterday?" He extinguished the thought that she'd made an excuse to see him, but not before feeling the tiniest bit pleased.

"Yeah, I forgot." But the way she chewed her lip and refused to meet his gaze as she got out of the car decreased her credibility. She fussed with her hair, shoving it over her shoulders as if it was a bother.

She seemed so uncomfortable, the woman of far too many words suddenly struck silent, and he scrambled for a way to relieve her discomfiture. "Did you come to monitor our progress? I can show you the roof trusses we've set. We've worked really hard. I promise."

"No, that isn't necessary." She shook her head emphatically. "I just need to get my things from the church so I can get over to Andrew and Serena's house."

"The Westins?"

Nodding, Charity took a few steps toward the door. "I talked to them this morning and promised to come over and play with Tessa for a while before I go to work. It's a big transition for her, suddenly having a brother."

So she hadn't come by to see him after all. He hated the disappointment that reared inside him, but that didn't stop him from wanting to delay her departure a few minutes longer. "It's nice of you to think of that little girl." Her blush deepened at the compliment.

"Tessa's really special. I teach her in Sunday school. Although she lives with a painful illness, juvenile rheumatoid arthritis, she's always smiling."

Charity gazed at the parsonage, her eyes shining a bit too much, but she rolled her lips inward and looked away a few seconds. When she faced him again, the shimmer of threatened tears was gone. Rick wondered if it had been there at all. It was the most honest expression she'd displayed since they'd met.

"Yeah, I've seen her playing on her swing set. She's always laughing," he said when she didn't speak.

He glimpsed the shine again before she turned to pull open one of the glass double doors. "You're sure you don't want a tour?" he said, relieved when she stopped again and turned back to him. "Or better yet, you could come back tomorrow, and I could put you to work on the crew. How are you with a pneumatic nailer?"

She laughed at that, the sound sweetly feminine. Melodic even. "I don't think you want to let me loose on society with one of those."

"That's too bad. I sure could have used a bigger crew, especially for framing. I only have eight, and a dozen would have been better. Faster."

Something akin to relief filled him when she allowed the glass door to fall shut and turned back to him. "Adding me to the crew would be like subtracting one of your regular guys. Maybe even two. They would have to work full-time to fix my mistakes."

"You'd be fine as long as you remember one rule. Measure twice, cut once." He demonstrated the concept with his hands.

"I'll try to remember that."

Levity glimmered in her eyes, tempting him to tell his best knock-knock joke just to see her laugh again. But he waited too long, and she reopened the door. "Sorry, I've really got to go." She waved and disappeared inside.

A few minutes later, after Rick had returned to the power saw, Charity crossed the parking lot and hurried to the parsonage. She emerged again with the petite curly-haired brunette, who danced rings around Charity as they approached the wooden play structure behind the house.

As much as Rick tried to focus on his own directions about measuring and cutting, he found himself watching them. First, Tessa slid down the yellow slide into Charity's open arms. Then, Charity stood and twirled around and around with the child's legs tucked around her waist. When both appeared sufficiently dizzy, Charity carefully lowered to the ground, and both rested on their backs kicking their feet up in the air.

The scene was so sweet and private that Rick felt it was an invasion to watch, but he couldn't make himself look away. Charity's laughter drifted across the lot on the few occasions when he turned off the saw and his crew took a break with the nailer. His chest tightened, the sound of their laughter threatening to wrap itself around his heart, but still he observed them.

Though she wrestled and laughed with Tessa, Charity moved cautiously, as if to protect the child. A nurse's instinct. Hospitals—Charity, working there, and Tessa, a frequent guest—probably were the common denominator connecting the two.

Before Charity had mentioned anything about Tessa, Rick had already known about the Westins' fragile child, the information courtesy of Rusty. If only his friend would stop telling him stories about the people at Hickory Ridge. It felt too personal.

He especially wished Rusty would stop talking about Charity. Without that information, Rick could have been just a casual observer now, one who might have guessed he was witnessing a tender moment between mother and child. But Rick knew better. And the knowing ruffled his thoughts even more. This was not her child but Serena's daughter. Serena, the woman who had taken what Charity had believed to be her place in Andrew's heart and by his side in church hierarchy. The youth minister's wife.

But the loving picture the woman and young girl painted together, still giggling as Tessa straddled Charity's belly and tickled her under the chin, revealed none of that uncomfortable history. The sides of Rick's mouth turned up in a smile he couldn't restrain.

For once, Charity was being benevolent and living up to her name. She was such a paradox. Just when he thought he had her figured out and could justify his resentment toward her, she allowed him to glimpse this other, endearing side. He wasn't sure how to process this observation, fearing he liked this side a little too much.

In what felt like a short time later, Charity and Tessa walked hand in hand through the back door into the house. Rick surprised himself by wishing she wouldn't leave so soon. The way she blurred the clear lines around his personal boundaries, he should have been wishing she would disappear until the building dedication instead of hanging around and distracting him.

From his perch on the ladder, Rick glanced at Charity as she climbed in the car. She looked over and waved shyly before closing the door. Despite his embarrassment over getting caught watching, Rick couldn't help wondering when he'd see her next. Or hoping it wasn't too long.

At work a few hours later, Charity tried to contain the smile that pulled at her lips as she yanked the shirt of her fresh scrubs over her head. Finally, she just gave in. It was amazing what a play date with Tessa and a civil conversation with Rick—especially that—could do for her mood. She'd sensed his gaze upon her several times as she'd played with Tessa, but she'd probably imagined that.

But she hadn't imagined during their earlier conversation that Rick had been pleasant. Nice even. It couldn't have stunned her more that he'd taken the time to discuss the child with her, and her cheeks warmed at the thought of his compliment.

As tempting as it had been to mention his comment about praying and to spring into a litany of questions, she'd resisted. She would have avoided anything to keep him grinning like that, with sunlight dancing over his eyes and dimples softening the hard lines of his face.

"The slow night doesn't seem to be bothering you," Dr. Walker said as they passed in the hall. "What's making you so happy?"

She raised an eyebrow at the young obstetrician she'd always enjoyed working with, but tempered her smile anyway. "Can't a person enjoy her job without having to withstand the third degree?"

"Guess not." The doctor chuckled as she headed down the hall in the opposite direction.

Farther down the birthing center hallway, Charity reached the nurse's station and the room-status board. Set up in a grid, that dry-erase board was nearly blank except for a few last names listed with MBV—for a mother-baby vaginal delivery—and MBC—for mother-baby cesarean section. She seconded Dr. Walker's prediction that it would be a light night.

Charity traced her hand along the wooden handrail that mirrored wood flooring. At the doorway to an empty LDRP room, she stood for several seconds before stepping inside. There she took in the dark wood, the rich colors of the wallpaper and the muted lighting that she usually didn't have the luxury of time to observe. Instead of the medical equipment she usually focused on, hidden behind wood cabinetry, she examined the sleeper chair that waited in the room's corner for another exhausted father.

The crib against the wall caught her attention. Inside its Plexiglas part referred to as a "bucket," she imagined a tiny baby squirming under the warm lights. She could see a nurse leaning over the crib, starting to "eye and thigh" him, inserting erythromycin in his eyes to prevent infection and injecting vitamin K in his thigh for blood clotting. Though those two jobs would have been automatic for her, she was strangely certain she wasn't the RN on duty.

Stranger still, she suspected *she* was the other woman in her daydream—the one resting on the bed with a man by her side. It was so close, this dream of hers, that she could almost grasp it. Could cradle the sweet baby against her heart. Could lace her fingers with those of the man who touched her hair so gently.

"Hey, Charity, quit daydreaming," Jenny Lancaster-Porter called from the doorway, grinning at her fellow labor and delivery nurse. "The clerk just put a walk-in in Room 224, and another mom's taking the chair ride from ER."

Charity jumped guiltily at being caught imagining things that were becoming closer and closer to impossible. But at that moment they hadn't seemed unattainable, not when for the first time, she'd imagined herself on the other side of the bed. The one with a family, with joy, with hope for the future.

Jenny snapped her fingers in front of Charity's face. "Girlfriend, are you coming? These babies can't wait."

On command, Charity's thoughts clicked into focus the way they always did, and she followed at Jenny's heels. "I'll take the walk-in. You take the chair."

Jenny winked. "Already wrote that on the board."

Both chuckled at Charity's attempt to hand the precipitous case to her friend and Jenny's hearty receipt of the gift. Jenny liked her deliveries fast and furious, and Charity didn't mind the occasional slow and steady, so they had developed a great working rhythm from several years of working shifts together.

"You'll be on dinner break, your patient and baby settled in for the night, and I'll still be walking the halls with mine," Charity said as she turned into Room 224.

Just the opposite proved true, with Charity's patient crowning within half an hour, and Jenny's walking the halls for two hours and eventually being sent home after a bout of false labor. Charity had barely had time to get a fetal heart rate and start an IV before the delivery, let alone to record advance directives in case something went wrong or to inquire about nursing or bottle-feeding.

The rest of the shift was equally unpredictable. It was as if every full-term mother who had avoided ruining her Labor Day barbecue had gone into labor just before dawn broke. Staying busy had prevented her from analyzing that earlier daydream. Or how familiar the man in her dream had seemed.

At least she didn't have to worry Jenny would tease her about catching her spacing out earlier. They'd become good friends, the kind who could be counted on to overlook little faults. Besides, as they passed together through the door that separated the birthing center from the rest of the hospital, Jenny looked exhausted enough to have forgotten the whole thing.

Rapid steps behind them had both turning back to their nursing supervisor, Kathryn Myers, with dread.

"Ladies, Becky and Theresa called in sick, so we're really tight this morning." Kathryn looked back and forth between them with what appeared to be pity before asking, "Can you work over?"

Her tired body hollered no, but Charity nodded, watching Jenny do the same in her peripheral vision.

"We're also short a scrub technician," Kathryn continued. "Charity, can you scrub in on a case?"

Because a few years back she had taken the orientation for scrubbing in on C-sections, Charity was occasionally called upon to do that type of work.

"I'm on my way."

She boxed away any remaining weariness as new energy flexed in her muscles. There would be plenty of time to be tired later. Right now the busy night they'd spent was about to become a busier morning.

Chapter Five

Rick stared up at the morning's threatening sky and wondered when he would ever catch a break. It was bad enough the holiday had stolen a day of productivity and it had poured all night, leaving the construction site a muddy mess. Now they probably would lose another workday to a storm. How would he ever finish this project on schedule, especially with the no-Sundays clause?

"Want to call it a day, Boss?" Rusty stared up at the same ominous sky, obviously drawing similar conclusions.

Rick climbed up on the picnic table, using the bench as a footrest. "No, let's wait a bit. You know how tight this schedule is. If it's not going to pour, then I want to make some progress today."

Rusty nodded and headed back over to the crew huddled around a dusty pickup, sipping coffee from foam cups. His foreman looked as antsy as Rick felt.

This work had to get done. Soon. Today. Yesterday, in fact. The electrician was scheduled to be in next week, and they didn't even have a roof on the building.

The crew gathered around two pickups, dangling their heavy boots off tailgates, probably sharing single-guy stories from the way they chuckled. Rick was a single guy, too, but bosses didn't fit well into those conversations. Besides, with a social life as empty as his, he had nothing to contribute, anyway.

Rusty ambled back over to him, apparently not fitting into those discussions, either. They took turns shooting nervous glances at the sky.

"Still wish you could have made it to the Labor Day cookout," Rusty said. "Those kabobs I made were out of this world. The kids missed you, too. Them and Tricia."

As much as he'd regretted missing the event, he'd needed a vacation day—away from everyone—as much as anybody. "Sorry I couldn't make it. Maybe next year."

"It's a date. And…you know…you could bring one."

Rick chuckled, though it felt forced, as he couldn't relax. "Do you have someone in mind? My bank teller just graduated from high school. My favorite waitress at Klancy's has blue hair and just celebrated her golden anniversary. I don't know anybody else." Okay, he did, but he wouldn't mention *her* now.

"Wow, you need to get a life," Rusty said, punching him in the arm.

"Thanks for the advice, buddy. I'll keep it in mind next time I'm running payroll."

Rusty patted him hard on the shoulder and stepped away just as the wind rustled the trees on the church grounds. "This work isn't going to get done by itself," he said, already tromping to the site. "It's not raining yet, and it might not all day. Why waste time?"

Rick looked up at the sky and doubted his foreman's weather-forecasting abilities, but he couldn't fault Rusty's logic. After a bit of employee grumbling, the crew followed the foreman and pulled back the tarps covering building materials.

When the familiar sounds of hammers and saw blades cut the morning's quiet, Rick finally sighed his relief. Perhaps his deadline wasn't so unattainable, after all. And maybe he was wrong in worrying that he'd be found out as the failure so many from his past had predicted he would be. Yes, indeed, things were looking up, for both R and J Construction and for Rick himself.

But the wind that lifted his hair just then made him wonder again. They were bound to get rain that day, sooner rather than later.

"Yo, guys, let's get the tarps back down," Rick called out as he jogged over and started the job himself. "Rusty, we need you down here."

"Sure thing, Boss. Just need a second to get a few more nails in."

"We don't have a second," Rick retorted, but his

words couldn't compete with the nailer's rapid-fire thuds just as the wind started to howl.

Whether Rusty heard Rick or not, Rick sure heard the loud grunt that came from the ladder the foreman already should have climbed down. Rick rushed to the bottom of the ladder, casting a furious glance at the other crew members, one of whom should have been steadying it.

"Aw, man…how could I…oh, the stupid…what in the world…aw, man." Rusty's string of unintelligible comments suddenly stopped. "Hey, R.J.," he said in a strained voice. "Could use some help up here."

"I'm coming," Rick said, already climbing the ladder, with one of the men holding it. When Rick got close enough behind him, he leaned over to check the damage.

A sixteen-penny nail protruded from the back of Rusty's hand, blood trickling slowly from the puncture. The foreman's other hand shook as he still held the pneumatic nailer, so Rick handed it down to a crew member.

"Let's get you to the hospital," Rick said as he held Rusty's arm and helped him down the ladder.

"Aw, man…I can't believe…aw, man."

Rick nearly smiled at the irony. Another man might have been swearing a blue streak by now, but Rusty held tight to his convictions. Just another thing Rick respected about his friend.

Finally, they reached the ground, and Rick bunched his old flannel shirt beneath Rusty's arm to catch the dripping blood. At least one of the men had thought to grab the shirt from Rick's truck. He would have taken that moment to yell about what someone had failed to do, but the sky decided to dump on them right then.

"When it rains, it pours," Rusty said with a tight laugh.

"You're right about that." Rick ushered him toward Rusty's truck while barking orders over his shoulder. "Chuck, you're in charge. Secure the tarps and load the tools in my truck box. Then you can head home. See you all tomorrow."

Then he climbed into Rusty's truck, shoving his dripping hair out of his eyes. He hoped to reach the hospital faster by taking the Atlantic Street route, avoiding Main Street and downtown.

"Now I know what the wood feels like." Rusty's laugh sounded more like a grunt.

"Are you planning to experience the saw next?" Like Rusty, Rick tried to laugh at a situation that was anything but funny. Even if the foreman's injury wasn't serious, it would still delay their work. They were already short on crew. Short on time. He refused to hear the voice inside that said, *You're always coming up short.*

"Thanks, Rick. For everything."

Why was Rusty thanking him when he was only focusing on his own problems? Bad friend or not, he observed Rusty's gray pallor and pressed the gas pedal harder. He couldn't decide which he'd rather do: slug him for getting himself hurt or hug him because he was okay.

* * *

"Charity, wait up," Jenny called, coming up behind her as she headed down the endless hallway toward ER and the hospital exit beyond it.

With dread, Charity turned around. No, she couldn't go back, even for the most critical case. She had nothing left to give her patients. The half moons under Jenny's eyes mirrored the exhaustion seeping through her own soul. She shook her head before the other nurse could get a word out. "No, not even another half hour. I'm toast."

Jenny laughed. "I'm not calling you back. I wanted to know if you'd thought about my offer to set you up with my brother, Brett. You remember, he just moved to Brighton. He's working there now."

"You know how I hate being set up."

"Yeah, I know. He hates it, too. But if you change your mind, let me know. Hey, want to go get a late breakfast or an early lunch?"

"Are you kidding?"

"I am," Jenny said, yawning. "No, I plan to be comatose five minutes after I walk in my front door. The storm won't be loud enough to keep me awake."

"Are the kids going to the sitter's today?"

Jenny nodded and moaned a sound of pure relief. Charity could relate, but she wouldn't find respite for herself until she crawled under her own covers.

Together, the two nurses passed through the nearly empty ER waiting room. The lone guest in a seat on the far wall caught her attention.

She barely recognized Rick at first, his hair dripping, dark T-shirt plastered to his skin. Thoughts of home and sleep disappeared, and she rushed over to him. "Rick, are you okay?"

He only shook his head and rolled his eyes—his contradictory message as confusing as it was frightening.

"Hey, what's going on?" Jenny said.

Until that second, Charity had forgotten her friend, who now stood staring down at a very soaked Rick. Charity turned to her. "Let me call you later. My friend Rick needs—"

"Hey, it's nothing," Rick interrupted her with a flip of his hand.

Charity was grateful for the interruption. How dangerously close she had come to saying, "Rick needs me." She had no idea what this man needed, but it definitely wasn't her.

With a quick glance at each other, the nurses turned to focus on the man in the chair.

"Hi, Rick," Jenny said finally. "I'm Jenny."

"Hi." His mouth formed a grim line.

Jenny glanced at Charity and lifted an eyebrow. "Call me," she said with a wave before heading to the exit.

Anxiety squeezed Charity's throat as she waited for Rick to explain. Why it mattered so much she couldn't begin to decipher. It had to be her emergency training kicking in. When she thought she would explode if he didn't speak up, he saved her the trouble and the mess.

"It was just a dumb accident," he began.

On cue, she scanned his soggy form for blood. A few darker stains spattered the front of his shirt. But where was the source? She glanced at his arms, down his wrists to ten work-roughened fingers.

"I can't believe Rusty did this…." He let his words trail off as if that explained everything.

If it did nothing else, it allowed Charity to release the breath she hadn't known she was holding. It wasn't Rick. He was fine. But then Rusty wasn't. Wait. What kind of person wished pain on someone to spare it for someone else? And why had she chosen to spare that particular someone?

The emergency room doors whisked open then, saving Charity from answering those difficult questions. Tricia emerged, her stride long, her sandals smacking the linoleum floor as she marched toward Rick.

When Tricia reached them, she turned to Rick. "What was he thinking?"

At that moment, it dawned on Charity that the woman wasn't worried about her husband. She was mad.

"He'll be okay." Rick reached out to squeeze Tricia's shoulder. "We got lucky and the hand surgeon was here on another case when we got here. He told Rusty the nail pushed all the tendons, nerves and arteries out of its way, so he's not going to have any permanent damage. The only concern now is infection."

"But shooting a nail gun through his hand!" Tricia

jerked away, her voice climbing with each word. "How ridiculous is that?"

So that was it. Charity was relieved to finally have the situation explained.

"It was an accident, Tricia. The doctor said he gets cases like that one all the time." When Rusty's wife started shaking her head, he added, "Besides, with the wind, one of the men should have been holding the ladder."

She only shook her head harder. "He's the foreman. He could have held the ladder instead of climbing it."

Rick shrugged at that, as if he might have thought the same thing. "After a few days' rest, he'll be able to come back to work, too."

"Great, so he can do it again." She sighed.

Rick looked up as Rusty exited the door separating ER from the waiting room, his hand heavily bandaged. Tricia turned and rushed up to her husband, hugging him on the opposite side from the injury. It was as if her fear and anger had battled, and her fear had claimed victory.

But then Tricia backed away and folded her arms over her chest. "How could you?"

Rusty reached his good hand to touch her arm. "Sweetheart, it was just an accident. My hand's going to be fine, praise God. The wind caught the ladder, and I lost my balance a little."

"You shouldn't have been up there like that, anyway," she said, backing away before he could touch her.

"It wasn't a big deal—"

"It *is* a big deal. One of these days you're going to get yourself killed, and then I'll never forgive you."

As if all the oxygen in the room was suddenly sucked out, they all fell silent. After several uncomfortable seconds, Rick moved closer to the couple who were having this very private conversation in public.

"I'm going to take off now. Rusty, you're in good hands, right?"

Rusty nodded, an embarrassed grin on his face. He dipped his head again. "Sister Charity."

Slowly, Tricia turned back to the two standing not five feet away. Her cheeks flushed red. "Sorry. It's been a long day…already."

"And getting longer by the minute." Rusty drew his wife beneath the shelter of his good arm, the earlier comment seemingly forgotten. "You two go on ahead. We'll hobble along just fine."

He didn't have to ask twice.

"Great," Rick said. "We'll see you later, then. I'll drop off the truck at your house." Placing his hand at the back of Charity's elbow, he ushered her out the emergency entrance. "Whew, that was close."

Charity tried to ignore the tingling on the back of her arm where he'd touched her. "That was too bad," she said when nothing more imaginative came.

"Yeah."

Neither said more, but he didn't seem to be in any more of a hurry to leave than she did. His reasons weren't clear, but hers were mission-oriented. Maybe she'd get another chance to invite him to church, especially in light of the accident that obviously had bothered him. But first she needed to say just the right words.

"Hey, do you think you can do me a favor?"

His question startled her out of her plans. That surely was the reason for that flutter inside her. "What…what do you need?"

"Would you follow me to Rusty's house so I can drop off his truck and then take me back to mine at the construction site?"

"You mean the church?" she said, knowing full well he did. "Sure…I guess."

Minutes later, as she followed him in her car out of the hospital lot, she finally let herself smile. Who knew mission work could be this easy? She was giddy with the *prospect* of having this particular prospect in her car, so she focused all her attention on convincing him he needed the church. It wasn't about being alone in a car with a man at all. A certain man.

She shook her head to focus her thoughts and tapped the brakes after coming up too closely behind the truck. Her mission was clear. All she had to do was stay focused on it.

Funny, earlier this had seemed to be a well thought-out plan. But as Rick parked the truck and watched Charity's car approach in the side mirror, he questioned his brilliance. The idea had been so practical. He'd needed someone to help him play the car-trading game. She'd been there. He'd needed an easy escape from witnessing Rusty and Tricia's argument. She'd been there. It was as simple as that.

Or maybe not.

If this whole thing could be summed up so easily, he shouldn't have felt any jolt when Rusty had said, ''You two go on ahead.'' *You two.* As if they were a couple or something equally ridiculous. Anyway, his foreman hadn't insisted they go on ahead *together.* No, Rick had initiated that all by himself. It wasn't because he just wanted to spend more time with her, either. He wouldn't admit to that, even under torture tactics.

As she pulled her car to a stop behind him, Rick ducked his head and yanked off his sopping shirt, pulling on a clean T-shirt that Rusty wouldn't mind him borrowing. For once, his friend's habit of keeping clean shirts in the truck and changing in the middle of the day didn't seem so eccentric. His decision to change, had nothing to do with the woman parked behind him.

Wet shirt in hand, he jogged back to her car, steady raindrops dampening another shirt before he could climb in. Charity, wearing blue hospitals scrubs he hadn't noticed until then, shifted uncomfortably in her seat and fussed with her safety belt. His clever car-trading idea was flawed, all right.

''Anyone ever told you you're a tailgater?'' he said as he clicked the door closed.

She glanced up, a blush scaling her neck. Strange

how it pleased him to know he had inspired that feminine flush.

Instead of facing him, she started the ignition and adjusted the mirrors. "Did anyone tell you that you drive slower than a pack mule walks?" Her face tightened, as if she was holding back a grin.

"The posted speed limit in the village is twenty-five miles per hour, and I try never to exceed that limit—"

"I doubt that."

"When I'm driving someone else's car," he finished.

"Oh…yeah."

"Besides, are you saying it's okay to break laws?"

"No, I'm not saying that. I'm just saying— Oh, forget it." She shook her head.

Because he liked this flustered version of Charity, he couldn't resist adding, "You are a tailgater, though."

"Okay, I'm a tailgater."

"You almost rear-ended me."

"But I didn't, right? The back bumper is just as shiny—or should I say rust-covered, in the case of Rusty's truck—as it was before this dangerous drive."

With a sigh, Charity pulled the car around the truck and pressed the gas a little too hard, making the car lurch forward. Rick grinned. It was good to know he wasn't the only one who felt rattled by this situation. Being this close to her, he could breathe in the antiseptic soap smell on her hands. The soap tried, but didn't succeed, in masking her light lavender scent. He squeezed his arms closer to his sides, hoping his damp, sweaty smell didn't make her pass out behind the wheel.

"Did you just get off work?" he asked to fill silence.

"I had to work overtime."

"I bet you're exhausted." Even as he said it, he noticed the purplish half moons beneath her eyes and the tiny red lines of fatigue surrounding the hazel color.

She shrugged. "It's not too bad."

He didn't believe her, but he didn't push the issue. "Just don't fall asleep and crash into a tree or something. I've seen enough of that hospital for one day."

But he hadn't seen enough of Charity. Hadn't he just decided he wouldn't admit something like that? Their verbal sparring matches entertained him. Nothing more.

They were passing that unusual new statue in the center of Main Street—the one with a wheel and swans—when Charity looked at the digital dashboard clock and jerked in her seat. Though they hadn't been sitting close enough to touch, she leaned closer to the driver's side door. Away from him. The confusing change didn't sit right with him somehow.

Her eyes still on the road, she cleared her throat and spoke. "You know, I am pretty tired. Would you mind if we stopped at Milford Baking Company and got some coffee and a doughnut? My treat."

"Doughnuts and anything free—two of my favorite

things,'' he answered, ignoring blaring warning bells in his mind. Spending more time with Charity probably wasn't in his best interest. ''But don't you need to get home?''

''I need sugar and caffeine worse.'' She didn't like how shrill her laugh sounded.

''Great minds think alike.'' If her great mind was thinking anything like his, she'd be changing her plans and dropping him off at the church as fast as her car could drive there. But when she parallel parked along Main and opened her car door, he couldn't help feeling relieved.

Chapter Six

Charity steadied her hands on the edge of the ice-cream-parlor-style table as Rick settled across from her. Trying to appear nonchalant, she took a first bite of her lemon-filled powdered-sugar doughnut.

"You had to pick the messiest doughnut in the whole case, didn't you?" Rick said.

She coughed and busied her hands, dabbing a napkin to her lips. "I can't help it. Lemon's my favorite."

"To each his own." He nibbled on his cinnamon roll.

Though they munched and sipped without speaking, the silence didn't make her feel nervous. Just the opposite, in fact. It was somehow comforting just sitting here with him, eating and noticing how his hair curled wildly after the downpour. He probably hated that, but she thought the curl softened his appearance some.

Rick took another bite of his roll and smiled contentedly. Despite her exhaustion, Charity couldn't believe how good she felt. Almost too good. Way better than she should have been feeling, especially when she'd only brought Rick there to avoid a misunderstanding. She'd made a split-second decision when she'd remembered it was Wednesday. Women's Bible Study didn't dismiss until 11:30 a.m. Mother never missed it, even scheduled her work at the investment broker's office around it.

And no doubt if she saw Charity and Rick together, Mother would assume something was going on between them. Incorrectly, of course. Still, it hadn't seemed right to subject her mother to such unnecessary worry. No, her choice to wait until study had ended would be better for all involved.

"Are you falling asleep over there?" Rick asked, drawing her out of her thoughts.

Charity shoved the hair that had slipped from her ponytail behind her ears. "I was just thinking."

"About the accident?"

Not really, but she could go with that. "It was too bad."

"Nah, Rusty wasn't hurt that badly. He was lucky."

She shook her head. "No. About that fight in the waiting room."

"Tricia didn't mean it. She was just scared and mad."

"Still, I was surprised. She's supposed to be a good Christian woman. In Ephesians, Paul tells wives to submit to their husbands as to the Lord and that husbands are the head of wives as Christ is head of the church.''

Rick shifted and planted both palms on the table. Still, his face appeared calm as he spoke. ''Didn't it also say in that same chapter, 'Husbands, love your wives, as Christ loved the church and gave Himself up for her'?''

Charity nodded in defeat of her point. Why did she even try making one with this guy, who always had the perfect comeback? ''All I meant was that right out in public she became angry and humiliated her husband—''

''Are you saying anger is bad? Wasn't there a time in the temple where Jesus was pretty mad at all the people who desecrated it? I think he demonstrated his anger publicly, too.''

Charity raised her hands. ''Okay, okay. I give.''

And instead of pushing his advantage, he shook his head. ''Why do we keep doing this?''

Her hands dropped to the table. She didn't have a clue. Irony, perhaps, in arguing Scripture with a man who didn't attend church. Deep in her chest she felt a rumble that became a chuckle by the time it reached her throat. ''I don't know. But can we quit already?''

''Don't you like a good Scriptural debate?'' He grinned when she rolled her eyes at him.

''Not when I always lose.''

He shrugged. ''You *always* start it.''

''Okay, I won't do it anymore. I promise.''

''And I'll stop winning. I promise.''

He must have tried to hold back a laugh, but he coughed it out anyway. Charity joined in with him because it felt so good, so authentic. Why did laughing at herself feel more honest than anything than she'd done in months?

The clink of the glass door opening gave her a welcome escape from those confusing thoughts. In dashed a preschooler who immediately pressed his nose to the sparkling display case. A harried mother, a baby attached at her hip, rushed in after him.

"That one, Mommy. That one."

The child pointed to a gooey concoction with sprinkles. To a wail of protest, the mother ordered two chocolate chip cookies, rummaging through her purse and producing a few crumpled bills. Tension showed in the tight pull of the woman's lips.

The whole scene made Charity smile. She wondered if the mother realized that some people watching might consider the moment poignant. The stuff that memories were made of. Would people observing Rick and Charity together get a different impression as well? Would they imagine a young married couple so in love that they'd slipped away from their jobs for a late-morning coffee break together?

Warmth spread in Charity's chest, forcing her to scramble for more logical thoughts. Of course, onlookers wouldn't imagine they were married, especially if they were close enough to view their bare ring fingers. For a few seconds she studied his rugged hands that were clasped on the table. They didn't have the clean, trimmed nails of the minister she would one day wed, but they were pleasant in their own way. Their small scars and calluses spoke of honest work, and their strength promised protection for someone he loved. Did Rick have someone to love?

With a furtive glance in his direction, Charity caught him watching her. But instead of the raised eyebrow and a discussion about dirty fingernails she would have expected from him, he averted his eyes. He couldn't have been staring, so Charity felt humiliated by the fleeting wish that he had been.

"You've got to be tired. We should go back so you can get some rest."

A glance at her watch confirmed her suspicion it was still too early to go back to the church, so she was grateful for the rain that continued to pelt the sidewalk outside. "You want to go out into that?"

Rick looked out the window and shrugged. "I didn't melt earlier, so I'll take my chances."

"Well, I might…melt that is. Let's wait to see if the rain lets up."

"Fine with me, but I'm still hungry." He stepped up to the counter and ordered, asking over his shoulder, "Want something? I'll buy this time."

Charity shook her head reluctantly, finally settling back in relief into the chair. She didn't want to leave, and not just because they needed to pass a little more time before returning to the church. Who could blame her for wanting to spend a little more time with a handsome man, even if friendship was the most she could ever expect from him? Or want from him, right?

When Rick returned to the table, he set another lemon-filled pastry in front of her. He waved away her protest. "Hey, I saw you watching the doughnut case. I'm just giving you another so you don't drool on mine."

Giving in to temptation, she took a bite. She followed his gaze when he turned to peer outside again.

"I'm not in any hurry to head back out into that, either. Another day of work…wasted."

"That must be so frustrating for you."

Rick only shrugged. "But, hey, I sent the crew home, so I can stay here until the rain stops, or as long as you want me."

Her sip of coffee must have taken a mistaken path because she choked right then, coughing several times into her napkin before she could stop. Obviously, he'd meant he could be there as long as she wanted company, but that wasn't what he'd said. *As long as you want me.* Her next choke barreled on top of the one before.

"Are you okay?" Rick said, rushing around the table.

Charity raised a hand to stop him and finally was able to stop choking. He'd returned to his seat and was grinning at her by the time she looked back at him.

"I thought I was going to have to give you the Heimlich. You're the nurse, not me. Are you all right?"

Her cheeks burned so hot that even her ears must have been red. "I'm fine." But was she really? No way could she call herself *fine* when she'd nearly asphyxiated herself over his offhand comment. As if he'd just offered to stay a lifetime and she was all for it, or something equally outlandish. And fine wasn't something she could call herself when she was purposely trying to hide this meeting from her mother— even if it would help avoid an unnecessary misunderstanding.

The cramped walls of the bakery seemed to tighten in on them, the round table between them appearing smaller than when they'd first sat. A few other customers milled around in the shop, but it suddenly felt as if Rick and Charity were alone there. It was too close. Too intimate.

Charity had to turn away. Instead, she focused on the preschooler who'd managed to smear more chocolate from his cookie on his shirt than he ever could have gotten into his stomach. Checking her watch again, she realized it was noon, a half hour past the end of Bible Study. The church parking lot should have cleared by then.

"It looks like the rain is letting up," she said, glancing at the weather outside, which, if anything, had gotten worse. "I really ought to get home."

Rick surveyed the outside himself and raised a questioning eyebrow but didn't contradict her as he cleared away their garbage and placed it in the trash can.

Raindrops splattered cold on her face as she stepped out onto the sidewalk but did nothing to relieve the heat in her cheeks. How foolish of her to have sat in the bakery, imagining things she'd had no business even considering. Rick McKinley bore no resemblance to the godly husband she'd planned for her future. And she needed to make that very clear to herself…and him.

After a quick, wet jog to her car, they drove in silence all the way back to the church.

"Thanks for the ride," Rick said as they pulled alongside his truck. "And for breakfast."

"You paid for seconds."

"The least I could do."

Relief covered Charity so effectively as he opened the car door that she tried to ignore the pang of regret she also felt. Her plan had worked. Everything had turned out fine. Mother wouldn't have to make any mistaken assumptions about her and Rick. Charity had gotten her wayward imagination under control. And she was one step closer to getting Rick to agree to come to church.

But as the glass church door flew open, her relief vanished faster than the lull in the steady rainstorm.

Rick glanced back at the banging door to see a vaguely familiar middle-aged blonde emerging from the church in a huff. Until then, Rick hadn't noticed a fourth vehicle parked in the lot in addition to his truck and Reverend Bob and Charity's cars. A Lincoln he'd seen there regularly. As the slight woman marched toward them, he felt an inexplicable urge to flinch.

But when she neared them, she walked right past

him, heading for the driver's side door. Charity had climbed out before the woman stepped up to the car.

"We missed you at Bible Study this morning, sweetheart," the woman said, although the endearment did little to soften her caustic tone.

"I worked overtime," Charity said simply.

Sprinkles of rain dampened Rick's skin as he stepped around the car to inject himself into the conversation. He felt oddly as though he should protect Charity from this woman he didn't even know.

"I see." The woman looked back and forth between them in a clear suggestion she believed Charity was lying.

A sudden need to deflect attention from Charity made him reach out his hand toward the woman. "Ma'am, I'm Rick McKinley from—"

"I know who you are," she interrupted, only looking at his hand until he lowered it. Almost as an afterthought, she said, "I'm Laura Sims. That is my daughter." She pointed at Charity. When she could have said, "I'm Charity's mom," she'd named her as a possession, as if her daughter were an old car or something. Disliking Laura Sims came easy to him.

And why had she staked the claim in the first place? Did she see him as a threat to her daughter? Or perhaps to her hold over her daughter? Hadn't Rusty said something about Laura Sims being domineering and training Charity to be a future minister's wife? Then Laura's behavior toward him made no sense. He was no threat to her plans. He and Charity were just friends. Barely that.

Laura faced Charity, turning her back to Rick. "Why are you here now?"

"There was an accident at the new building this morning, and Rick had to take Rusty to the hospital. I'm just bringing him back to pick up his truck."

"Oh, Reverend Bob mentioned something."

"Rusty's hand is going to be fine," Rick reported, annoyed Laura hadn't even asked.

Without responding to him, she spoke again to her daughter. "You're probably exhausted. You should be at home in bed."

Instead of here with this unacceptable man, she might as well have added since it couldn't have been more obvious. If he hadn't figured it out by her words, then the message Laura presented him by continuing to keep her back to him should have cleared up any lingering doubts. He was extraneous to the conversation, but that didn't stop him from hovering and listening.

"Mother, why are you still here?" Charity finally asked. "Didn't Bible Study end at eleven-thirty?"

At once the pieces of the morning's puzzle fit tightly into place. Charity had planned their little breakfast to avoid having her mother see them together. Resentment over being made a part of Charity's duplicity made him see the justice in her getting caught. But he still had the strange urge to throw his body between the deceiver and her nemesis. Instead, he shot a knowing glance at Charity and caught her peeking back at him.

Laura turned just in time to catch the exchange and

crossed her arms over her chest, glaring at them both by turns before focusing again on her daughter. "You know what time Bible Study ends. You haven't missed Wednesday morning Bible Study in what…six months?"

That jab had been clearly more for Rick's benefit than Charity's, and he knew it. The message was clear: *This woman is off-limits to you.* Couldn't Mrs. Sims see he wasn't interested in her daughter?

After a pregnant pause, Laura continued, brushing her damp hair back from her face. "I just had to stop by Reverend Bob's office to give him some suggestions regarding his sermons."

Charity nodded, as if accepting those words at face value, but Rick had no doubt those "suggestions" were criticisms. Reverend Bob, the good man Rick had come to know through Rusty's endless stories, was probably nursing a wounded pride in his office. *Like mother, like daughter.* Rick shook away the impression. Not even Charity could be as bad as her mother seemed.

"We'd better get in our cars before we're all soaked," Charity pointed out.

"Yeah. Thanks, Charity. I appreciate the ride." He turned his head to Laura. "Nice meeting you, Mrs. Sims."

He didn't expect her to answer, and she didn't disappointment him. As he strode away from them, Rick heard Laura's next loud comment.

"It was nice you were being a Good Samaritan,

but next time could you think to call your mother first instead of leaving me to fret?''

Rick kept right on walking, but he glanced back to see Charity, her hands held wide in a plea for understanding. She was apologizing for being with him, and he was surprised by how much he resented the fact. Laura's defensive pose, arms crossed and chin jutted in a startling contrast to Charity's contrite demeanor, rankled him as much as the woman's selfish comment.

Since when were people punished for doing good? Were good deeds only to be done for the *right* people? Hyprocrites. He just couldn't seem to escape them.

He fired up the truck's engine and drove out of the parking lot, waving at Charity as he passed. She didn't wave back, obviously too busy defending herself to her accuser. Rick couldn't get away from that fast enough. The strange thing was he had the insane temptation to take Charity away with him.

Rusty already had his good coloring back and was piloting the remote when Rick visited him Friday night. If not for bandages that kept him from scanning the channels with his usual speed and dexterity, he was back to normal. Too bad it would be a few weeks before he would be able to operate machinery again.

''This is the life, isn't it?'' He used his good hand to flip the lever and recline his chair.

Rick chuckled, not buying one bit of his best friend's act. ''You're going nuts, aren't you?''

"Yup. They're going to have to strap me in and cart me away if I have to *relax* another day. How does somebody relax with three ruffians running around?"

As if on cue, two-year-old Max scrambled through the living room, two red balloons following him down the hall. On his trail were four-year-old Rusty Jr. and their sister, Lani, just a year older.

"Hey, that's my balloon. Give it back," Rusty yelled.

Lani paused midstride and galloped to the sofa. "Hi, Uncle Rick." She used the nickname the children always called him, although they weren't related, as she scrambled up to his lap. After their hug, she hopped back down and rushed back through the kitchen.

"Mom." Lani stretched out the word until it sounded like two syllables. "Max popped his balloon. Now he's taking ours."

A tired-looking Tricia appeared at the doorway, pressing her hands against the door frame. "Relaxation. I've often wondered that myself," she said, answering Rusty's rhetorical question she'd obviously overheard.

But her grin showed no rancor as she ignored the scuffle in the other room and crossed the floor to hug Rick. Then she settled on the arm of Rusty's recliner and kissed the top of his head. Her husband set aside the remote and reached his good hand to caress her arm. Clearly, their argument had blown over, and they

were back to being the near perfect couple Rick remembered.

A squeal of pain from the back bedroom brought
Tricia up from the chair. "Better go referee," Tricia
said, already on her way down the hall.

Rick turned back to Rusty. "Cabin fever?"

"Of the worst kind, but Tricia and I came up with
a plan to cure it. Sunday night, since the evening service is canceled, we're having a week-past-Labor-Day
potluck here and inviting the church crowd." He
watched Rick intently for a few seconds. "Hey, you
should come, too."

"Thanks for the invite, but I have to…"

"Keep thinking, buddy. You'll come up with a
good excuse." But Rusty said it with a ready grin.

"You know how I feel about—"

"I know," Rusty interrupted. He barely took a
breath before adding, "So how's Sister Charity?"

Rick had taken real punches that stung less than
that verbal blow. "What do you mean?" he said
when he finally got his bearings again.

"The two of you left the hospital together. Any
developments I should know about?" He waggled his
eyebrows in that way he often did when he wanted
to be annoying.

"She took me to drop off your truck, and we got
some coffee. End of story." Okay, so it wasn't the
end of the entire story but the end of the one he was
willing to tell.

"Did you meet Sister Laura, then?"

"At the church. Yeah." *Her and her invisible baseball bat,* he longed to add but refrained.

"She's a pill, isn't she?"

"A whole bottle," Rick couldn't resist adding.

Rusty nodded without humor. "I just wish she'd give Sister Charity more breathing room."

"It's as if she wants to relive her perfect life—before widowhood—through her daughter. As if Charity doesn't have any choice in the matter." When Rick spoke the words aloud, he was surprised by how strongly he believed them. And by how much the situation bothered him. More than disliking the way Laura pushed her daughter around, he hated that Charity wouldn't—or couldn't—stand up for herself. She needed someone else to stand up for her, then to teach her to be her own best advocate. Funny, he'd never thought of himself as the white-horse type, but here he was tempted to don some armor.

"I think you're right," Rusty answered, studying him.

Rick stiffened, caught pondering help for the woman who annoyed him as frequently as she entertained him. "Not much anyone can do about it." Quickly, he stood, ignoring his friend's knowing grin. "I'd better get going. See you Monday?"

"I'll be there—about half-useful but there."

"Tell Tricia and the kids goodbye for me."

Outside the tiny white bungalow, Rick could finally breathe again. But even the homey accents of forest-green shutters and geranium-filled planters on the porch failed to calm him. He could leave behind

Rusty's outlandish assumptions about him and Charity Sims, but the perplexing thoughts and the need to just this once do something heroic about them, he took home with him.

Chapter Seven

Charity awoke late Saturday morning to the sound of muffled voices at her front door. At least it seemed like morning, though the high sun peeking in her window suggested otherwise. She couldn't have slept more than an hour or two after getting off work.

Curious, she wrapped a lightweight bathrobe over her nightgown and jogged down the stairs.

"You're awake after all." Rick smiled up at her from the doorway. The white bakery bags in his hands contained something that smelled delicious.

"Probably from the noises down here," Laura said sardonically before frowning back at her daughter.

But Charity wasn't listening for false cheeriness or sarcasm in either of their voices. She was too busy wishing the floor would gobble her up and forget to burp. It was the first time she'd seen Rick since that embarrassing scene on Wednesday, and she hadn't had a chance to apologize for involving him in that confrontation with her mother. With a day shift on Thursday and another seven-to-seven Friday night, she'd had little chance. But she hadn't tried too hard, either.

Humiliation must have been what had her heart tripping. Still, she cringed at how she must have looked—like something the cat dragged in and then tossed back out. Lifting her hand, she patted her sleep hairdo and then tightened the belt on her robe.

It shouldn't have mattered what he thought of her, but the fact was it did, and she was too nervous this morning to even try to find proper justification for it.

"Hi, Rick," she choked out. When she reached the bottom of the stairs, she looked from Rick to her mother for an explanation. Laura's stiff posture showed that no matter what the meeting was, it hadn't been her idea.

But Rick didn't seem to notice as he took another step into the entry, with only Laura between the two of them. "I wanted to thank you for breakfast the other morning. It was so nice of you to take me out after Rusty's accident. I just wanted to return the favor."

How fortunate that Mother had opted not to replace her problematic teeth with dentures because the way her mouth hung open, she would have dropped the set on the tile. Charity barely kept her own mouth closed. From the sideways glance her mother tossed her, Charity understood that her mother now knew another detail she'd failed to mention from the other day. That outing had seemed so minor a detail in the scheme of things, especially since Laura had already been giving her the silent treatment over the misunderstanding.

"You really shouldn't have...." She let her words trail off as nothing could add to it. No, for all their sakes, he really shouldn't have come or told.

Rick raised one of his two bag-covered hands as if to interrupt, although she'd already stopped talking. "Of course I should have. I'm just repaying a kindness. Anyway, I brought your favorite. Lemon-filled."

Charity's cheeks burned as she brushed sweating hands down her robe. Her mother's disapproving gaze felt hot upon her. Rick had made a point of declaring that he knew one of her preferences, leaving the idea open that he might know others. The question was, why? "That was really nice of you, but—"

"I know it's a little late for breakfast, but, as far as I'm concerned it's always time for doughnuts."

Charity stepped toward him. "They smell delicious."

But Laura moved so she was more solidly between them. "Thank you, Mr. McKinley, for bringing them by."

Shock had Charity jerking her head to face Laura. Would Mother really accept the gift from him and shut the door in his face? No, that wasn't possible. Mother would never be that rude. But when Laura took hold of the bags, Charity lost every bit of that confidence.

"You have to stay and have some with us," Charity said, stepping past her mother. "It looks like you brought enough for an army—and a hungry one at that."

Rick's warm laughter filled the room with music. Either he hadn't noticed Laura's rudeness, or he'd decided to ignore it. "Yeah, I overdid it. Everything looked so good in those glass cases."

"Of course you'll join us," Laura said as if it had been her idea all along. It probably had been. "Come in and sit in the dining room while I start some coffee and my daughter gets dressed."

Dismissed and annoyed at being commanded around like a child, Charity jogged up to her room and tossed on a sweatshirt and her favorite worn jean shorts. She'd barely made it back down the stairs before her mother called her into the kitchen. The pocket door that separated the room from the dining room—the one always left open—was firmly closed. And, as she'd guessed, the coffee carafe, their china cups and saucers, linen napkins they never used, sugar bowl and spoons were already arranged on a tray.

She'd seen the look of disappointment on her mother's face too many times to fail to recognize it now, so she steadied herself for the onslaught.

"Why is that young man here?" Laura said in a voice just above a whisper.

"He just said—"

"I don't care what he said. I want to know why he's really here."

"He's *really* here to bring us breakfast and to thank

me.'' Even Charity heard the frustration in her voice that caused her mother to raise an eyebrow.

Why did she suddenly remember the visit of another young man—the dinner they'd coerced Andrew into? Her mother had supported that visit wholeheartedly. But this situation didn't resemble the other at all. Rick's dropping by had nothing to do with securing a good match with a man of God, even if she privately questioned her earlier assessment of Rick as ''ungodly.'' She now knew he prayed. And he could quote the Scriptures with the best of them.

Still, she wished her mother wouldn't have made such a big deal about his visit. Whether or not Charity had been reluctant to tell her mother about the favor she'd done for Rick, that still didn't excuse Laura's ungraciousness.

''Mother, we must be compassionate. Rick's probably just lonely since Rusty's convalescing. I don't think Rick has many friends, so we should be kind to him.'' When Laura didn't uncross her arms or soften her stubborn expression, Charity added, ''It's the Christian thing to do.''

At once, Laura softened but still eyed her daughter suspiciously. ''As long as that's all it is.'' Laura lifted the tray and waited while her daughter opened the door. ''Now then, Mr. McKinley.''

''Call me Rick...please.''

At the point where the older woman might have said, ''Please call me Laura,'' her silence spoke for her. After a few long seconds, Laura glanced down at the bakery bags resting on her antique lace tablecloth. "Sweetheart, could you bring that china platter and the dessert plates from the counter, so we don't have to eat right from the bag?"

Charity obliged, trying to ignore the unpleasant knot forming inside her gut. She must have heard wrong. Had Mother suggested Rick's gifts weren't good enough because they came in a bag? Or had Laura meant that Rick wasn't good enough? Shaking that thought away as foolishness, she sat opposite her mother, with Rick between them at the head of the table. As soon as Laura had arranged the assortment of doughnuts, turnovers and cinnamon rolls, Charity selected a lemon-filled.

"We mustn't forget grace," Laura said after the others had taken a bite. She quickly corrected their faux pas.

"Amen." Rick took another bite of his cinnamon roll.

Charity dived back into the pastry, wishing it were a lot larger, so they could eat longer—silently. But Laura took only one bite of her jelly-filled and set it delicately on the plate before turning to Rick.

"It has been a short work week for you with the holiday, hasn't it, *Mr. McKinley?*"

Rick looked up and met Laura's gaze directly, as if he sensed an impending attack. "Not really. I worked Monday. Your daughter was there. Didn't she mention seeing me?"

The sweet concoction in Charity's mouth caught in her throat, causing her to cough several times into her napkin. "Yes, Mother, I saw Rick there, but I was busy trying to get some of the fall planting finished.'' Having the good sense to realize it wasn't the time to mention that Rick helped with the planting, she only hoped he didn't feel the need to confess.

''I take it you and Rusty are friends.'' Laura took a sip of coffee while she waited for his answer. Her pastry sat on the plate, forgotten.

Well, at least her mother had picked an innocuous subject like Rusty. Everybody loved him. The subject wasn't quite as bland as what Rick liked about Milford—the one Charity would have voted for—but close.

Rick nodded. ''Anyone would be lucky to have a friend like Rusty.''

His succinct answer caught Charity off guard. And it had her revisiting feelings she'd hidden from since the day at the bakery. She had become Rick's friend now, too. Would he one day say something as sweet and loyal about her? Or would she wish for something even more personal?

''Rusty sure does love the Lord,'' Laura agreed. ''He and that young wife of his, as well.''

They were all in such accord that Charity half expected someone to start a chorus of *amens* soon. Still, something didn't feel right in all that harmony, as if a discordant note were on the verge of being played. Rick must have noticed it, too, for he stiffened. The knot inside Charity inflated to a soccer ball.

Laura dabbed her already clean lips on a napkin. ''That young man is such a huge asset to Hickory Ridge Community Church. A trustee, volunteer lawn manager and Sunday school teacher. I'm sure it's just a matter of time before he's elected deacon.''

"He's already been nominated once but wasn't elected that time," Charity added if only to delay her mother's segue into another discussion of her father.

Laura continued as if her daughter hadn't spoken. "That young man is so much like my late husband. Charity's father was truly a godly man, providing so well for our family, even after his passing, God rest his sweet soul. Did Charity tell you her father was a deacon?''

Rick barely got a yes out before Laura continued. The rest of the story, which Charity could have repeated by heart, continued as background noise as she replayed all of her conversations with Rick, concluding she'd never mentioned her father to him. Charity's ponderings of why he would have said otherwise melded with her mother's voice and words like *loved the Lord* and *accepted the call* until Laura's last comment snapped her back to reality.

"One day, my Charity will find a godly husband just like her father.''

Charity turned to see her mother's syrupy smile. Her own face felt glued into a neutral position, while she feared at any second her jaw would drop open and reveal the shock that spread through her body in waves. The message couldn't have been clearer if Laura had written it on the tablecloth with a marker: *You are not good enough for my daughter.*

Why was Mother doing this? She had to know that Charity would never consider dating a man who didn't go to church. So why was she saying all of these embarrassing things in front of Rick? Humiliation had a taste, Charity discovered, and it was the soured remnants of the sweet lemon flavor on her tongue.

Rick appeared unruffled by the conversation as he took a long draw on his coffee. "How nice for you both."

The way Laura's eyes narrowed tempted Charity to throw herself across the table to protect Rick—an impulse she didn't want to explore.

Charity nearly clapped her hands with joy when her mother finally changed the subject and asked Rick questions about his company's other projects. It seemed like safe territory, even though Rick had already confessed to being worried his company wouldn't make the construction deadline. She hoped for all their sakes that a miracle would happen so the church family could be in the new building for the Thanksgiving celebration.

"Who is the *J* in R and J Construction?" Laura was saying as Charity reentered the conversation.

Rick chuckled at that, a stilted, flat laugh that sounded nothing like his earlier laughter. "The *J* is for Jon. My name is Richard Jon McKinley."

"That's right. Rusty introduced you as R.J., but then corrected himself," Charity added before she could stop herself and earned Laura's censoring glare.

"He's the only one who calls me that."

Hearing irritation in his voice, Charity only smiled. If her trying to befriend him and looking out for his soul bothered him, then he'd just have to live with it. She wasn't about to bail out on God's plan. Her project to bring Rick to church made her feel useful, something she hadn't felt in a long time.

"So in other words you're saying that you misinform the public by allowing your clients to believe you have a partner when you're the sole proprietor?"

Laura's words scattered Charity's focused thoughts. Did her mother consider this conversation a compassionate way to treat someone she wished to see in church? Before long, Laura probably would do something unthinkable like declare Rick a heathen bound for hellfire.

But Rick handled the game of twenty questions easily, pushing his chair back and resting with his hands on the chair's arms. "You're right. I guess I have. But anyone who's signed a contract with me or has inquired about my partner knows the truth. At the time I just thought the company name sounded better."

"I like the way it sounds," Charity chimed when she had a chance to break into the conversation. And because she couldn't help being curious, she added, "Did you ever consider starting the company with a partner?"

He shook his head. "I'm not really one much for partnerships." The sadness in his eyes seemed to indicate that he spoke of associations of any kind.

"Oh," was all she could say. In the conversational lull that followed, Charity finished the last bite of her doughnut and reached for another. Why did what he'd said—or what he hadn't said—bother her so much? She wasn't looking for a relationship with him, anyway.

If things were different, if *he* were different, then maybe… That silly daydream she'd had at the hospital flitted through her mind. Of course, Rick wasn't the man from her dream. She probably wasn't even the woman she'd imagined resting on the bed. So why did a lump form in her throat that the sweet baby in the crib wasn't theirs?

Perhaps to fill the silence, or maybe because he felt compelled to explain himself, Rick continued. "I had never found anyone I could be partners with. Well, Rusty, maybe. But he likes being foreman."

"I'm sure he appreciated the gesture, though," Charity added, trying to keep the conversation from dying again. Besides, talking helped her to avoid confusing thoughts. Her search for a proper spouse was part of the straight-and-narrow path she'd chosen, so she had to avoid wrong turns at all costs.

Laura's coffee cup clinked as she set it back in the saucer. "You'll both have at least one project to be proud of when you complete the Family Life Center."

"You're right." Rick cleared his throat and stared out the window facing the wooded back yard. "I hope we finish on time since this job is so important to Rusty."

"It's important to the whole church body," Laura said.

"It doesn't help that Rusty's injury will keep him

off the job a few days. He'll come back Monday, but he'll only be able to supervise for a few weeks."

"That must be frustrating for you both."

As she listened, Charity released the breath she'd been holding. Mother had finally come to her senses and decided to give poor Rick a reprieve from her harsh game. *How unlike Mother to be so unkind.* Charity tried not to acknowledge the voice inside her that listed other instances when Laura had been just that. Like when they'd first learned that Reverend Bob's daughter, Hannah, was pregnant and had refused to reveal the father's name. Anyway, who was Charity to talk with her own judgmental past? Like mother, like daughter.

But it was the mother's words—not the daughter's—that struck like a hammer to the center of the antique cherry dining room table.

"I haven't seen you at church, Mr. McKinley. Do you attend somewhere else?"

Rick's relaxed posture immediately stiffened again, and he crossed his arms. "I don't go to church."

Laura straightened, as well, shock and disdain clear in her expression. "Why is that? Are you working on our church and yet not a believer?"

He met Laura's gaze directly, the muscles in his jaw clenched, aggravation apparent in his squinted eyes. Charity had seen that look before, directed at her.

"I have a problem with organized religion overall. Churches tend to have too many hypocrites for my taste." He never addressed Laura's second question.

"Well, I never," Laura said, as if Rick's accusation had been addressed at her, probably a good assumption.

Rick stood and pushed in his chair. "On that note, I should be going. Thank you, Mrs. Sims, Charity, for an enlightening morning. Enjoy the rest of your weekend. I'll see myself out."

What Rick had said was reprehensible, so why didn't Charity feel compelled to give him the dressing-down he deserved? She couldn't possibly believe he'd been justified in saying those things.

Laura didn't speak but loaded dishes onto the tray and carried them into the kitchen. She'd left the platter of remaining pastries on the table, apparently dismissing the gifts along with the giver.

Well, someone in this house has to have manners. "Thank you again for the pastries," Charity said, seeing him out. "And thank you for coming by."

Rick nodded, his gaze apologetic. He pressed his lips together and hesitated, but he must have decided against saying whatever was on his mind because he only shrugged. As he opened the door, he turned and waved. Then he stalked to his truck and backed out of the drive.

Regret over a nice visit gone bad had an empty ache settling inside her chest. That was all it could have been. Allowing herself to have feelings for Rick would only bring pain to her, to him and even to her mother. She refused to let herself believe that unnecessary pain had just begun.

Chapter Eight

"Stay away from Mr. McKinley," Laura announced as she put the last of the flatware in the dishwasher and wiped her hands on her apron.

Though Charity had been expecting her mother to say something, she still jumped. "Mother, I don't—"

"Of course, you don't know what you're doing, letting a man like him come around." She bent to dump the platter of pastries right in the garbage. "That man is so inappropriate for you."

Shame over her mother's earlier behavior transformed in a flash to exasperation. "Why would you say that, Mother? I'm not seeing Rick. We're only friends." She took a small satisfaction in using his Christian name that her mother had avoided. If they were having a conversation about him, they could at least use his name.

"You heard him. He's an unbeliever. Isn't that

enough for you? You don't need any *friends* like that.''

''That is ridiculous—''

''It's not ridiculous. There's no reason for you to surround yourself with people like that. Unbelievers. He blasphemed against our Lord.''

''No, he didn't. He only said he disagreed with *organized* religion.''

''I know what Mr. McKinley said—he's not like us. You have no reason to be around him, threatening your own spiritual walk.''

How could her mother be so judgmental? Laura seemed to have forgotten Jesus' gospel commission to make disciples of ''all nations''—a sweeping term that obviously even included Rick McKinley. Still, stranger than her mother's closed-minded attitude was the way Charity felt so threatened by it. Hadn't she shared many of Laura's perceptions only a few weeks before? What had changed?

But no, this wasn't about differing opinions. This was about Rick. And Mother was wrong about him.

Charity planted her hands on her hips and faced Laura. ''Rick never said he didn't believe in God. Besides, even if he were a unbeliever, isn't he just the type of person we should be reaching out to?''

Laura's eyes widened for a few seconds but then narrowed. ''Charity Lynne Sims…''

What is wrong with me? She'd never questioned her mother's opinions before. She needed to show more respect. Her mother had lived a lot longer than she had and had learned many things she couldn't begin to know yet. She needed to listen to that experience.

"I'm sorry, Mother. I should never have spoken to you that way."

Laura's expression softened. "I should think not. I don't know what's gotten into you lately." And then she smiled. "Of course. Why didn't I think of it before? Helping to deliver the Westin baby weighed more heavily on you than we first thought."

"That has to be it," Charity agreed.

Laura nodded in that way mothers do when they're certain they're right. "And as for Mr. McKinley, are you more interested in saving his soul or making his home?"

The comment struck like an unexpected slap, but Charity tried not to flinch and give away her own confusion. "No, Mother, that isn't it." She shook her head hard as much to make her point as to stop the *Hamlet* quote from repeating in her ear, "The lady doth protest too much, methinks." "I just feel that God wants me to be the person to bring Rick to church."

Laura hung the towel just so on the refrigerator handle before turning back to her daughter. "There are plenty of others in our church who have more critical needs than that young man. How about young Hannah? She could use help with her child while she studies. Though our situations are so different—she's, of course, an unwed mother, and I was widowed—I remember the challenges of raising a child alone."

"I know, Mother. Being a single mother was really

hard on you. But look what a great job you've done.''
Charity spun around, grateful for a chance at silliness
in a morning that had been anything but uplifting.

Laura touched Charity's hair, which she'd tied back
when Rick had arrived. ''Yes, I think, with the Lord's
help, I've done a good job. I thought I'd never get
over the grief of losing your father, but I had you to
raise.'' Laura paused and glanced wistfully out the
window. ''You gave me a reason to get up every
morning.''

''Yes, we were lucky to have each other.'' Charity
said it because she needed to agree with her mother
at least once that day.

Laura smiled, as nostalgia seemed to overtake her.
''Did I tell you how excited your father was to start
New Testament class at the seminary before the ac-
cident?''

A million and one times now. The unkind thought
shouldn't have surprised her. Sometime between last
night and this morning she'd become an awful daughter who didn't have a single nice thing to say. ''Yes,
Mother. You've told me. You must have been so
proud of his choice.''

''We mustn't be prideful, but I did find a certain
joy in being the wife of a godly man. You'll find that
same joy someday soon, sweetheart.''

''I'm sure you're right.'' Maybe voicing it out loud
would give her the confidence that had been in short
supply.

''Your father would have been pleased with the
choice I'm sure you'll make. He would have loved to

escort you down the aisle into the hand of that perfect groom.''

Charity gasped. Daddy. It didn't matter if she had to strain for any memory of him beyond baritone laughter and the strong arms of a safe embrace. She still couldn't bear to disappoint the image she'd created of him from the yellowing wall portraits. She longed to see approval in his eyes when she wed the man God had planned for her.

And if everything she'd always believed were true, the man would be a godly one. She'd spent years preparing for her calling as his equally godly wife. She'd studied, volunteered and taught. She could play the piano and the organ. Didn't all ministers' wives play the organ?

Suddenly, she felt more committed to that mission than ever. Joseph Sims had been a good example, even if she had to get her stories about him second-hand. She wouldn't allow herself to be a disappointment to Daddy, who surely watched her from Heaven, by selecting a mate who could not match the expectations he would have had for her. Settling for anyone less than that perfect choice—even someone like Rick—was out of the question. But even as she recommitted herself to that lifetime quest, she wondered if anyone could measure up on that impossible yardstick.

Sunday morning Charity scanned the church, its pews appearing oddly empty, despite the crowd of regulars taking their seats.

The fifth pew on the south side, where Rusty and Tricia usually sat with their children, remained vacant, as usual. They were always late.

Other congregation members sat in their regular places. Robert and Diana Lidstrom were in the second pew on the north side, with Darla Ann Brewster right behind them. Even new member Mary Nelson had already developed a habit of sitting just two rows behind Charity and Laura's second-row pew on the center aisle.

"How are you, Laura?" Head Deacon David Littleton asked as he and his wife, Judith, took their regular spots just down the pew from the Sims ladies.

"I've been busy, but I'm getting along."

"Lovely ladies' luncheon you planned," Judith said.

"I enjoy doing it. I like staying busy." Laura returned to her weekly study of the bulletin.

As more members took their seats, Charity became increasingly irritated. Nothing ever changed here. People came and went, sermons were spoken, altar calls given, but everything stayed the same. Her heart felt as empty as it always did. *Do something different. Say something different.* She wanted to yell it over the PA system. Yet she remained seated, just like everyone else. Just as unchanged as they were.

She refused to answer the voice inside that asked why she'd memorized the habit-formed seating chart when she couldn't remember any of Reverend Bob's sermons. Instead, she scanned the crowd mentally reciting their names.

But the name that kept resurfacing in her thoughts belonged to an individual she probably would never see sitting in one of Hickory Ridge's pews. Especially after his run-in with Mother the day before. She didn't want to give up on her calling to bring Rick to church, but she was feeling less convinced of her eventual success.

"I wish those youth members would hush," Laura whispered.

Charity glanced toward the rambunctious bunch in the last few pews. Sure enough, Brendan Hicks was at the center of the trouble. Giggles reverberated off the glass that separated the sanctuary from the vestibule. Again, nothing had changed.

"I'm sure they'll quiet down when the service starts."

"Someone needs to take those young people in hand," Laura whispered again. "Andrew should insist they sit with their parents if they can't behave."

"But you're glad the teens are here, right, Mother? You're glad they're hearing God's word, aren't you?" Charity whispered back, needing to know.

Laura rolled her eyes when Charity glanced at her. "Of course, dear. Don't be silly. But in my day, those who misbehaved or dared to fall asleep in church felt the business end of a switch."

The good ol' days of church attendance. Charity barely had time to tuck her tongue in her cheek before she felt guilty for that thought. She had to stop being mean.

Carrying an infant car seat and pulling along a kindergartner, Serena moved to join the merry band from the youth group. The whispers and giggles soon died down.

"Hi, Miss Charity," Tessa said in a loud whisper, earning a *shhh* from her mother.

Charity waved at them. Serena waved back, making Charity feel grateful again for her forgiveness. She wondered whether she deserved any kindness from the woman she had once humiliated in front of the whole congregation.

No, she wouldn't worry about that this morning. She'd try to listen to Reverend Bob's message this time. Maybe a rousing, Satan-stomping sermon would revive her spirits and remove that uncomfortable feeling that surrounded her lately in church. This was supposed to be her favorite place. All her friends were here. Certainly, her whole social life revolved around church. So why was she so unhappy in her favorite place?

"Good morning." Charlene Lowe, who'd recently taken over as music minister, asked everyone to open their hymnals for the call to worship.

Over the flutter of turning pages, Charity heard the Williams family rushing to their seats. Reverend Bob and Andrew climbed up on the platform and took their twin seats near the lectern, just as Charlene started to sing.

"'I come to the garden alone,'" Charity sang as loudly as usual, but lyrics she'd sung so many times suddenly bothered her. How alone she sometimes felt in this sanctuary filled with believers.

She hoped the minister's sermon would be an easy one. But her optimism dipped when Reverend Bob asked the congregation to turn to a certain passage in the gospel of John, the one about the woman caught in adultery.

"What did Jesus say to the Pharisees and the scribes who brought that adulterous woman before him?" The minister paused. "He said, 'Let him who is without sin among you be the first to throw a stone at her.'"

She'd thrown stones in her past, all right. Out of jealousy. Out of humiliation over coming in second place to a divorcée. Too much guilt had Charity searching for an escape—to the creaking sounds of children wiggling on the pews, the rip of someone tearing out an offering check.

The next words she heard from the microphone were those of Charlene asking everyone to turn in their hymnals for the invitation.

"Now that was a great sermon," Laura said after the benediction. "I'm really looking forward to the potluck tonight at the Williamses', aren't you?"

"Yes, it sounds like fun." Charity hoped she sounded convincing. Really, she wasn't convinced of a single thing in her life right now. Other than maybe that nothing about it seemed right.

Charity tried to gather some enthusiasm late Sunday afternoon as she and her mother followed the walk up to Rusty and Tricia's house, carrying covered dishes of Laura's locally famous scalloped potatoes and cherry pie for the potluck. Though the church's best cooks probably had brought their signature dishes, she wasn't even hungry.

For no good reason, she scanned the cars already lining the narrow side street, looking for a truck that wouldn't be there. Even if he was Rusty's best friend, Rick would take a ten-mile detour to avoid attending any activity that involved their church.

"Charlene offered to take me home so you'll have the car when you stay to baby-sit," Laura said as they climbed the front steps. A note on the door directed them to the backyard.

"Oh, that will be great."

"Where are Rusty and Tricia planning to go later?"

Charity shrugged. "Maybe a show in Novi, or they might just get coffee. With their three little ones, they don't get out very often as a couple."

"It was good Christian service of you offering to watch their children so they could have some time alone."

Charity didn't answer her as she tromped to the side of the house. Sure, she'd offered free baby-sitting as an act of service. But her work today was more than that. It came tangled up with confusing guilt over the comments she'd made about the Williamses' argument and the strange way Rick had put her in her place.

As they reached the fenced-in backyard, delicious smells and squeals of delight invaded her senses, leaving no room for either guilt or lingering questions.

"Hi, Miss Charity," Tessa yelled as she scrambled over from the back porch. "I saw you at church today."

"I saw you, too. Did you make those big kids behave?"

"Uh-huh." Tessa nodded enthusiastically. "I'm a big helper with Seth, too. That's my job. I'm a big sister."

Charity brushed her hand through Tessa's curls before the child darted off into the crowd of children.

The women settled their dishes on the paper-covered banquet table alongside chicken and noodles, someone's secret recipe potato salad and baked spaghetti. As Charity surveyed the growing crowd, taking in familiar faces, she caught herself searching for a tall form with bronzed skin and a head of light brown hair. Instead, she saw the tawny-headed Williams children charging across the yard.

"Miss Charity, Miss Charity," Lani and Rusty Jr. sang in chorus as they passed.

Hot on the trail of the younger kids were middle-schoolers Brendan Hicks, Steffie Wilmington and Chuck Donovan, although Brendan could well have been chasing Steffie, or vice versa.

Turning back from the racing ring of children, she caught sight of Tricia heading down the steps, arms laden with a huge lemonade container, and Rusty balancing a casserole dish in his healthy hand. Two of the men stepped forward to relieve them.

Hannah Woods followed them out the door, a squirming infant in one arm and a container of cookies under the other. Serena followed close behind her, carrying a pink frosted cake in a tall container.

The woman's trim figure made it seem impossible she'd delivered an infant so recently. Just over a week. So much had happened in those eight days since Charity had helped with that delivery…and met Rick.

Shrugging off the thought, she approached the food table. "What can I do, ladies?"

"Here." Hannah pressed tiny Rebecca into Charity's arms. The infant started wailing, but her mother popped a pacifier between her lips, and she was content again.

Charity ran her fingers over the six-month-old baby's blond fuzz, still a year shy of fitting in a ponytail. "Hey, Hannah, that's a cool trick."

"I'm never without a few of those," Hannah answered.

Swaying with Rebecca perched on her hip, Charity watched as Hannah finished arranging paper plates, napkins and plastic cutlery. She still looked so young despite the fact that she was eighteen and technically an adult. Having her baby had made her grow up fast. Sure, it had been rough for a while when Hannah had first gotten pregnant, but Charity had come to respect the young woman for taking her job as a mom seriously.

"How's college going?" she asked when Hannah caught her watching.

Excitement lit the teenager's eyes. "I've already started my first semester. I love my classes."

"I'm glad. You must be so proud of yourself."

Hannah blushed but didn't stop grinning. "You know Mary Nelson, who used to be Serena's neighbor? She's caring for Rebecca when I'm at classes or studying. The baby already loves her just like a…grandma." The young woman's voice caught on that last word, providing a reminder that Hannah had lost her mother four years before.

"Rebecca's lucky," Charity said. "She has a grandpa who adores her. She'll probably have Reverend Bob so wrapped around her finger that she'll get to swim in the baptismal pool." She was glad the widower had a granddaughter to spoil since he often seemed lonely when he wasn't tending to his flock.

"Only with water wings," Hannah agreed.

"I'm so glad everything is working out for you to go to college, Hannah. With Mary around, you won't have to worry about how Rebecca's doing all day, and you can concentrate on making the Dean's List."

Hannah laughed at that. "I'll try, anyway."

Charity laughed with her, but then gave in to the temptation to look past her and scan the yard again. Everyone was there, except the one person she wanted to see.

"I wonder if Rick McKinley will come." Hannah kept an awfully straight face for someone who seemed to know too much for her own good.

"Why would he?" Charity said as casually as she could.

"Rusty invited him." The young woman accepted her daughter back into her arms. "You know, Rusty really respects Rick as more than a boss. Tricia told me Rick bailed them out financially several years ago when they were really in deep."

Hannah turned, watching Charity a bit too closely, her stare too intense. The other woman didn't give it away in her expression, but Charity sensed Hannah knew about her secret interest in Rick. Perhaps someone clinging to her own secrets so tightly—the unnamed father of her sweet baby—could relate to Charity hiding from hers.

Finally, Hannah continued the story. "Later, when they tried to pay back the loan, Rick wrote it off, saying their getting their lives together was payment enough."

"I didn't know that," Charity said.

Hannah started toward her father, who had just arrived, but turned back to answer her. "Rick doesn't want anyone to know."

I didn't know, she repeated to herself, suddenly convinced of how little she knew about Rick. Already, she'd seen so many layers of mystery in him, all compelling her to study him more deeply.

In fact, Rick had been stealing into her thoughts with amazing regularity. More disconcerting than that was that lately her world only seemed right when he was around.

Chapter Nine

The magenta reach of the setting sun had lost its grasp on the horizon by the time Charity sat in the wooden living room rocker, cradling a snoozing Max. The last of the church members had taken their empty dishes and gone home, leaving Rusty and Tricia to their night out and Charity to her evening with the children.

"Miss Charity, will a whale swallow me like Jonah?" Rusty Jr. asked a fifth question since he and Lani had sprawled on the floor to watch a Bible story video.

"No. But, as Jonah learned in that story, it's important to obey God."

"Just like we should obey Mommy and Daddy," Lani chimed. "Do you obey your Mommy and Daddy? Or don't grown-ups have to do that?"

Charity's choked laugh caused Max to startle in his sleep before settling again. Did she intend to obey her mother, especially regarding a certain gentleman? "It's a little different when someone is all grown-up, but it's important to respect your parents," she answered, choosing to give an incomplete answer.

Because the child seemed to accept that vague response, Charity turned to look out the window, escaping more questions and her guilt. That was when she saw someone coming up the walk. The increase in her pulse and the tightness in her chest registered his identity as quickly as she could take in body size and shape.

Rusty Jr. must have approached the rocker silently because suddenly he was standing there, watching out the window. "Hey, it's Uncle Rick."

Lani joined him, and together they jerked the front door open, slamming it against the wall. The commotion startled Max awake, and he let out a wail of protest.

In seconds, Rick had pushed inside and stood before the chair. "Is everything all right?"

"Max just woke up, and he's not real happy about it."

"Oh," was all he said, taking several deep breaths.

Max glanced over with a furrowed brow before snuggling back against Charity's chest and closing his eyes. When she looked up from the child, Rick was smiling down at her, sending a shiver of happiness up her spine.

"Why are you here?" she whispered when she was sure Max had fallen asleep again.

"Rusty called earlier. I told him I would try to make it by later."

It's later, all right. She forced back a smile at the thought. Rusty probably had invited him to the pot-luck, and arriving after the fact was his compromise.

"Well, you've come just in time to help get the kids to bed." She stood up from the chair, nestling Max's head against her shoulder.

"Then I timed it right."

Charity shot a glance at him, but he was watching the children instead of her, so she couldn't search his face for the meaning behind his words. "Okay. I'll go put this one to bed. Could you read those two a story?"

"Sure." Rick dropped back on the couch, with Rusty Jr. immediately snuggling up to his side.

Lani flipped off the television and beelined for the bookshelf, returning with a thick book of fairy tales. Surprisingly, Rusty Jr. didn't argue with her choice.

The sweet image followed Charity as she carried Max to the airplane-papered room he shared with his brother. Obviously, the Williams children adored Rick. And their parents had accepted him into their personal lives, even with his unusual thoughts about organized religion. Maybe they, too, hoped to one day see Rick beside them in church. And maybe Mother really was wrong to forbid her to spend her time and her energy for the church outreach on this man.

Max awakened again when she lowered him into his toddler bed, so she sat next to the bed, rubbing his back until his breathing settled back in slumber.

The sight that greeted her when she returned to the living room made her fight back a chuckle. Rick sat upright, looking wide-eyed and trapped with sleeping children under both of his arms. Rusty Jr. had even slung an arm over his midsection. The big book must have slipped off Rick's lap, because it lay upside down on the floor.

Rick grinned at her and whispered, "Help."

She attributed the flutter inside her belly to observing that sweet yet utterly masculine scene.

"Are you going to help free me or not?"

Charity lifted Lani, grunting with the load.

"They're like a sack of potatoes when they're asleep," Rick said as he peeled the little arm off him and resettled the boy in his arms. "Remember, lift with your legs, not your back."

"Thanks for the tip. She's like dead weight." She shifted Lani and carried her down the hall.

They crossed on her return trip as Rick carried the steamroller of a preschooler, who appeared dwarfed in his arms. Rick's shoulder brushed hers as they passed.

Ignoring the tingle that tapped from her neck to her wrist was impossible. So she made herself useful by picking up action figures and fashion dolls in the living room. What would she say to Rick when he came back, and only the two of them remained in the room? Her stomach muscles tightened with prospect of being alone with him.

And they squeezed even more with that reality only minutes later. Their gazes caught and held as he stood in the doorway and she looked up from her place on the floor. Immediately, she stood. Silence only added to the tension, and Charity longed to defuse both by finding something to say befitting the moment. But somehow "We're all alone here, aren't we?" didn't seem the best choice to staunch the crackle of electricity.

Rick glanced past her, and she turned to see headlights as a car pulled up. "They're home."

Not a moment too soon, something deep inside Charity told her. She wouldn't even allow herself to contemplate what might have happened or have been said if not for the interruption. "That's good. I need to get home, anyway."

Rusty was first to step through the front door. "Hey, Rick, you made it. Thanks for coming by."

A silly grin appeared on his lips, either from the date they'd just ended or from the scene into which they'd entered. Her face warmed over the second explanation.

Rick gave a stiff shrug, his hands clasped behind his back. "I don't think I was needed. Charity seemed to have it all under control."

"Just the same."

Realization settled heavily in her heart. Rick hadn't shown up late to avoid the potluck. He'd come because she was there. Or at least to lend her a hand.

"Are the kids in bed?" Tricia asked.

"Just now," Charity said and cringed inside.

"Well," Tricia answered with a long pause, "thank you so much, Charity, for offering to do this for us. It was a kind gesture.'' Then she turned to Rick. ''And thank you, too. You've been great…as always.'' Releasing her husband's hand, Tricia stepped to Rick and, on tiptoe, kissed his cheek.

Charity watched that tender moment of grati-tude…wishing. Silly thought. She had to get ahold of herself. She didn't really wish Rick McKinley would kiss her. That was the last thing she needed.

As they stepped onto the porch, a cool breeze caught Charity's hair, putting her on notice that fall was coming. She blamed the weather for the chill in her spine. Luckily, Rick had been staring across the street and didn't notice her shivering. His truck was parked behind her car.

''Wow, what a night,'' Charity said to fill the void as they headed down the walk. ''Watching kids sure takes a lot out of you.''

He only grunted his agreement, so she had to juggle the conversational ball again. She was tempted to say something clever to delay their departure, but she knew better. She needed to say a quick goodbye and drive home. It had obviously been God's will that Rusty and Tricia would interrupt her single moment alone with Rick. Perhaps it was a sign, reinforcing her mother's warning.

''Thanks for coming by to help me,'' she told him, resigned to doing the right thing even when it wasn't her choice. ''I'll see you—''

But he spoke up before she had the chance to speak her vague goodbye. ''Do you want to go somewhere and talk?''

*   *   *

Charity looked as if she'd just been frozen in stone, standing motionless in the street. Of course, he'd shocked her with his question. He'd stupefied himself. What had he been thinking, asking her to go somewhere with him, when he should have been headed straight home? When he shouldn't have come in the first place?

The longer she took to answer, the more agitated he became. Obviously, she would say no. He should never have asked. "That's a bad idea. You don't have to—"

"I'll go." She said it confidently, though she looked anything but.

At least they had something in common. He felt no more certain of this situation than she obviously did. The only thing he was sure of was that he didn't want to be alone tonight, and for some inexplicable reason, he wanted to be "not alone" with Charity.

When he opened the truck door for her, she got in but pressed her side closely against the passenger door. Her discomfort reminded him of another ride a few days before. But they'd smiled together, laughed together even, since that first drive. She should have been at least a little more comfortable with him. And yet she wasn't.

Her mother had to have something to do with Charity's anxiousness. Laura's dislike for him was obvious. Again, he cringed over the control that woman had over her daughter. Still, Charity was a full-grown

woman who could form her own opinion about him—
if she only wanted to.

"Where do you want to go?" Charity said,
straightening as if she'd finally decided she wanted to
be there. "How about the gazebo downtown?"

Rick couldn't reconcile the relief that collected
around him in a blanket of warmth. "Won't it be too
cold?"

"No, it's nice out." But she shivered as she said
it.

He pulled his heavy, hooded sweatshirt from the
back seat of the extended cab and handed it to her.
The Henley shirt he wore would have to be enough
for him because he didn't have another jacket. "Here,
wear this."

"Thanks." She put it on just as they pulled into
the downtown parking lot that extended behind a row
of Main Street shops. Thirty feet away from their up-
front parking space, a white gazebo stood in a bricked
garden area between two businesses. Beyond it was
a fountain that hadn't spit water for several years.

Charity jogged ahead of him, reaching the gazebo
and climbing its steps. For once, village maintenance
people were a step ahead of the vandals determined
to profess their love, and the whitewashed building
shone beige in the soft light that dangled from the
gazebo's center.

"I love this place," Charity said, sitting on the rail.
"It's beautiful here at this time of night."

"You mean after all of the skateboarders have gone
home to bed?" He sat on the rail a few feet from her.

Her chuckle felt like the greatest reward in that he'd finally set her at ease. She shivered but only drew his sweatshirt closer around her shoulders. The ancient jacket made her appear so small, so different from the Amazon loudmouth he'd first met on the project site. Her golden beauty finally didn't seem in contrast to the gentle woman before him.

Charity wondered what he saw when he watched her like that. She snuggled deeper into his jacket, a combination of his masculine scent and sawdust wafting to her nostrils. That scent comforted her, endearing instead of unpleasant.

"Rusty was in good spirits today," she said.

"He'll get to come back to work tomorrow, but he'll hate having to stay out of the action."

Charity watched him straighten with the admission. "His accident set you back on the building schedule even more, didn't it?"

He only nodded and watched the headlights of a car driving along Main Street. She'd seen the way Rick worked, how important it was for him to do a job right. If only she could ease his frustration and extend his deadlines.

"It's just one more thing." His sigh hinted of more delays and headaches. "Maybe it was too soon. Maybe we weren't ready for commercial work."

He didn't elaborate, and Charity got the feeling he didn't want her to ask, so she didn't. They sat in silence, the air between them heavier than even July's best humidity. When Rick finally spoke, Charity jumped.

"Sorry about how I behaved with your mother."

Charity swallowed hard. They had both been in that room, enduring the same conversation, but obviously they'd seen it differently. "You have nothing to apologize for."

"Yes, I do. I purposely baited her."

"How can you say that?" she said, shaking her head. "Mother was just awful to you. I couldn't believe it. I'd never been so ashamed—" Her words caught in her throat as she realized how vehemently she defended him against her own mother. She was a horrible daughter.

His strange expression showed her betrayal of family hadn't gotten past him. "Either way, I'm sorry."

She laughed at that, the sound and fullness inside her chest relaxing her for the first time since she'd climbed into his truck. "It seems that all we do is apologize for bad behavior. Why don't we quit, okay?"

"Apologizing?"

"No, quit behaving badly." She laughed again. It felt good to laugh. "We could work on being friends instead. Deal?"

"Deal." He scooted closer and held out his hand.

Her mistake was letting him grip her hand. Charity trembled inside following the handshake that had lingered too long to be casual. She should have been relieved when he slid his fingers away, but she missed the warmth and comfort of his touch.

"…I really do, you know."

Charity glanced back at him, her cheeks burning

with the humiliation of being caught thinking tender but unacceptable thoughts. "What were you saying?"

"I said I do believe in God."

"I know you do."

Rick jerked his head, drawing his eyebrows together in a perplexed expression.

"The praying at church...the excellent command of the Scriptures," she said, pausing until he looked up at her. "It all added up." She waited for his nod before continuing. "What is your problem with organized religion, anyway? You never really said."

"Let's just say my experiences in churches haven't been good ones."

"What do you mean?"

"The people I met in church when I was a kid were more worried about who saw them at services than about what they learned about God there. And everybody was too busy condemning everybody else to have any time for reaching out to help others."

Charity pressed her lips together. "Churches aren't all bad, you know. A lot of good goes on in them."

The way he cocked his head to the side stripped away her tenuous calm. Did he know something she didn't? Did he know how she'd been questioning her faith lately, how lonely she felt? She wondered if he realized that while she sat with an open Bible in her regular pew, just a heartbeat away from the altar, she felt alone.

"I know that. There are some good people in churches, too. Rusty's one of them."

"There are others." She grinned. "Maybe you've

had some negative experiences at church before, but why don't you give it another chance? You're an adult now.''

''Rusty keeps saying that.''

''And he's right. Maybe if you try it, you'll experience the blessings you've been missing.'' She'd been missing them, too, not twenty feet from the baptismal pool. ''Can we expect to see you at church, then?''

His only answer was a shrug, his focus on the wood between his feet. But then he quickly looked up and met her gaze. ''So what's the deal with you and Andrew Westin?''

He did know. Her cheeks burned as humiliation overwhelmed thoughts of mission work. ''There's nothing between us. He's a married man.''

''Before that. I heard some interesting stories.''

Hopping down from the rail, Charity stood at the wide entrance, holding on to the post and looking out toward the street. At anything but him. ''The old spinster stories must make for good laughs in our congregation.''

''You? A spinster? Hardly.''

''I'm twenty-nine,'' she said without glancing back.

''So? I'm thirty-three. What does that make me?''

She looked back that time. ''In our double-standard world, that makes you a confirmed bachelor.''

His chuckle drifted up the back of her neck as he came to stand behind her. ''I guess that's true. But you're wrong about being a spinster.''

"How's that?"

"Spinsters are much, much older, and they don't…look like you."

Charity gasped but tried to cover it with a cough, awkward enough to convince her she had no future in acting. Had he really just said that, or had she just imagined it in her best daydream?

"I'll wear a tight bun and reading glasses next time," she said to diffuse the tension. But his nearness, just inches away from her as he rested against the other post at the entry, made her lungs feel tight. She needed to put some space between them, needed to avoid the temptation to lean closer so her arm would brush his.

"Do you really want to hear the Andrew story?" She returned to sit on the rail, wishing her insides would stop quaking. No, she didn't want to tell it, but it gave her something to talk about—think about—rather than moonlight and romantic gazebos.

"It's none of my business." But he sat next to her again.

Instead of looking at him, she studied the way the streetlights landed on the building next to them, flashing off the stained-glass pictures in the Wind River Gallery's display window.

"When Andrew came to our church, it was a big deal." She paused and choked back her awkwardness. "A nice single guy without any visible warts, who just happened to be a youth minister. There aren't too many of those around."

"Guys without warts or youth ministers?"

She looked for mirth on his face, but he wasn't laughing. "Both, I guess, but I meant young ministers. Even the deacons here have been married since the sixties."

"And you weren't prepared to break up any marriages?"

This time the sides of his mouth turned up. Because pacing seemed to be the only way to get through this story, she stood. "I was convinced Andrew was *the one,* so I tried to convince him, too. Even after Serena started attending our church, and I saw the way he couldn't stop looking at her. The way he never looked at me."

Instead of the "You don't have to tell me the rest" she'd been hoping for, Rick crossed his arms. Waiting.

Dread slowed her, but she continued to walk, if only away from memories that still shamed her. "I invited him over for a party that was really just dinner with Mother and me. I even passed off Mother's cooking as mine."

"You mean you lied?"

Her laugh sounded flat to her ears. "Mother said it wasn't really a lie because she intended to teach me to make every dish we served. And she did right after that." But Charity paused under the weight of long-carried guilt. "Yes…I lied."

"That's the whole story?"

Charity shook her head. "Then there was the day that I kissed him and earned the 'just friends' speech."

"It sounds awful."

Rick stood and took a step toward her, as if to comfort her, but she stopped him with her words.

"That's not the worst of it. When he chose Serena over me, I accused them publicly of having an affair."

He slowed. Who could blame him? She didn't deserve his pity or his compassion. But then he stepped closer.

"Was it worth it?"

His question haunted her, but it came with a strong hand that he rested on her shoulder. His gentle action pushed her close to tears.

"No. But I just couldn't understand why it didn't matter to him that she was divorced and a mother."

"He obviously loves her." He squeezed her shoulder once more and released it.

Why had the embarrassing situation seemed insurmountable when Rick could put it in such simple terms? "I think he does," she said, finally turning to face him.

"So that's it, then. You have to marry a minister or a deacon, right? Like your dad."

The last he didn't pose as a question.

"Yes, like my father, I guess."

Rick tilted his head and watched her.

"Has your mother told you a lot about your dad?"

"Of course she has."

"Did the two of them have a good marriage?"

Charity studied him the way he seemed to be studying her. "Yes," she answered vehemently. But did she really know that about her parents' marriage? Of course it had been happy. Otherwise, why had Mother always spoken so lovingly of Daddy? "Why would you ask that?"

"Did your father even have a first name? Why doesn't your mother ever use it?"

"That's ridicu—"

But he didn't let her finish. "Does she ever call him anything besides 'Charity's father' or 'my late husband?'"

Charity opened her mouth to contradict him, but closed it with a click. *Your father.* The words repeated in her ears. She'd heard them so many times before. "Maybe she still can't say the name Joseph Sims aloud because losing the love of her life still hurts too much."

"Maybe." Rick paused, seeming to contemplate her assertion. "And you're hoping your choice of a minister or deacon will be as successful as your mother's, right?" He didn't wait for an answer before continuing. "Then that's perfect. I'll never fit the bill, so that much is settled. We can be friends without ever worrying about a relationship."

Then why did this *perfect* situation seem so flawed? He'd just agreed to give her what she thought she wanted, but the gift box felt too light to contain a present.

"Great." She injected enthusiasm into her voice. "I'm glad that's settled."

But the concluded matter still hung heavy as they returned to the truck, sadness squeezing in as the third passenger. With the establishment of this great new friendship, they certainly didn't have many stories to share during the short drive back to Charity's car.

She should have been thrilled by his offer, especially since it gave her the inside track to be able to change his views about churches. Why did it feel as if his friendship wasn't enough?

Charity shoved the thought aside as she climbed behind the wheel, focusing on the dark pavement between the twin light sprays from her low beams. She needed to direct her thoughts singularly on the straight-and-narrow path her life needed to head. Rick McKinley didn't fit in the schematic she'd drawn for her future. He didn't possess the qualities she wanted in a husband. Or needed. So why did she suddenly feel so cheated by her own plans?

Chapter Ten

Rick dropped into bed later that night, his own weight and the weight of his confusion settling heavily on the mattress. He hadn't bothered to turn off the hall switch, so now a triangle of light sneaked into the room. It illuminated emptiness that went beyond a lack of furniture.

Why had the sparse contents of only a bed and chest of drawers never bothered him before? And why did it suddenly bug him so much now that he couldn't sleep?

He was kidding himself if he believed his discontent involved only bare windows and unpainted walls. Even if the room was filled with bedside tables, mirrored bureaus and a recliner, he still would have felt alone here. But the feeling that parked like a car on his chest only magnified his worries. *You're a loner who can no longer bear to be alone.* Rick chuckled at that irony.

His talk with Charity earlier had proven he'd lost sight of the border that had always separated and protected him from others. The line blurred just when he needed to reinforce it. No, he hadn't begged her to come with him to talk, but he sure had been relieved when she'd accepted.

Even now he couldn't explain why it had been so critical that she stay with him. Had it been just to share conversation, physical space and oxygen with another human being? He wouldn't allow it to be more than that.

So what had he been thinking, telling her that spinsters didn't look like her? Did he *want* her to be attracted to him? That would mean admitting an attraction to her, which he wasn't about to do. Charity was a study in extremes. Her appearance bordered on perfect; her opinions redefined the word *critical.* A moderately attractive woman would have been more his style, one with milder opinions or more diplomacy in sharing them.

Strike that. He didn't need *any* woman in his life. The fewer complications, the better. And Charity Sims was about as complicated as they came.

Admittedly, he'd glanced at her lips a few times, wondered what it would be like to kiss her, but he'd never claimed he wasn't human. Only someone made of stone could have avoided noticing her delicate mouth.

Rick shook his head, hoping to send those stray thoughts away, but her image still kept him company. Getting used to that would be a mistake. He couldn't rely on her—or anyone—to relieve his loneliness. That job he had to leave to God alone. *Father, I need some backup here. We're really getting behind on the project. Please lay Your divine hand on us this week, helping us to do our best work. And help Rusty's hand to heal quickly.*

Having petitioned for those needs, he prepared to close, but a sudden need to toss up a prayer for Charity took him by surprise. Away from church, did she feel she could approach God the way he did? He sensed that she didn't and immediately pitied her. Had she created her sanctimonious facade to hide fears and insecurities every bit as crippling as his own?

"And, Lord, be with Charity," he said aloud. "Let her know You're there. I don't think she knows it."

Laura never stayed up past ten o'clock, so as Charity came through the garage entry, she wondered why her mother had picked tonight to break that habit. Charity yawned, wishing she had more time before facing her.

In the living room, Laura glanced over the top of a book she probably hadn't been reading. "Sweetheart, it's past midnight. You had me worried. I didn't think you'd be home this late."

"The potluck continued a while even after you left. Rusty and Tricia needed at least a few hours alone."

Laura's book closed with a snap. "You mean they just got back? That was taking advantage of your generosity."

"No, no. It wasn't like that." Charity chased away the misunderstanding with her words, still searching for a way to avoid revealing the whole story. "I just stayed to talk awhile."

"You should have let them rest instead of wasting their time chatting. They have three little ones to care for, and Rusty has that injury to contend with."

Charity nodded but could finally breathe again. That second misconception would have to stand, at least for now.

"You're up awfully late," Charity pointed out. "You must be tired. I know I am."

And guilt had drained her energy even more in the last five minutes. She headed upstairs after saying good-night, her feet feeling heavy. Technically she hadn't lied, but her reticence had painted that gray area with an awfully wide brush. When had it become okay to mislead her mom? *When Mother was wrong.* Her mind's answer to the question only confused and shamed her more.

Once she'd closed her bedroom door, she shook her head to clear it. There was no excuse for lying. But not doing the right thing was equally inexcusable. Rick needed a friend, and she liked being needed.

She couldn't ignore her mission of ministering to Rick. But she wouldn't lie to her mother about it, either. She would tell her when the time was right.

"You're wrong about Rick, Mother," she practiced in a whisper. But the knot in her gut hinted that this "right time" to tell her whole story might never come.

* * *

Blaring music provided a backbeat for the instrumental combination of power saws, nail guns and hammers late Monday morning as Charity carried more pots of mums from the parking lot to the church building. The tunes sounded suspiciously like those she had denounced on the same site just over a week ago, but she didn't feel the energy to take offense. Maybe she'd softened.

The building site was aflutter with activity as workers carried sheets of plywood up the ladders while others pounded the boards into place on the roof. Rusty, one of his hands still bandaged, stood at the bottom of the ladder, appearing fidgety and annoyed.

Reverend Bob stepped out the door just as Charity settled at the flower bed near the main entrance.

"Good to see you this morning, Charity," he said as he stopped behind her. "Just heading out for a nursing home visit. It looks like you're adding more fall color today."

"Fall planting is taking longer than usual this year."

"I'm sure our members will appreciate your efforts." He dug in his pocket for car keys. "I know I do."

As the minister walked away, Charity glanced up to see Rick on the ladder, the nail gun in his hand beating out an irregular rhythm. He would probably drive himself twice as hard this week to make up for Rusty's lost productivity.

Returning to her own work, Charity dug her hands

into the cool earth, but her gaze kept stealing back to Rick. The memory of his determined face hid in the dirt as she planted, but she still found comfort in the constancy of plucking weeds and placing plants fifteen inches apart. By the time she sensed Rick's approach behind her, she was surprised at how much she'd accomplished.

"Oh, hi," she said, standing and wiping dirty hands on her jeans. "You've been working hard this morning."

He lifted an eyebrow but didn't call her on the fact that she'd been watching him. "We'll finish sheathing the roof today. Once we've got the building enclosed, the subcontractors can finally get their work done."

He looked down at the buttery-colored flowers she'd just planted. "You've done a lot, too."

"I've been busy."

"You didn't mention you'd be here this morning."

"I didn't think about it." And she hadn't—not when she'd been so nervous and excited, so confused by the feelings he inspired in her. Now she occupied her busy hands by crouching low and collecting her tools and empty black containers. He squatted beside her to help.

"There are still so many weeds." She grabbed a handful. "I thought I'd gotten most of them last week."

"Okay, weed terminator, I'll let you get back to work." With a salute he returned to his own project.

With the day growing warmer, Charity shed the sweatshirt she'd worn to fight the morning chill in favor of the T-shirt beneath it. One by one the men's shirts came off and became tool belt accessories. Some men larger, some smaller, some darkly tanned or sunburned, none of the crew appeared as fit and strong as their boss. The last to remove his shirt, Rick pushed himself harder than the rest. He reached higher and hammered harder, as if a punishing task-master dwelled within him.

She wished she could say something to slow his self-destructive bent that kept the muscles in his shoulders and arms in constant flex. If only she could convince him that pushing himself wouldn't make up for the series of construction delays.

His shirt was back in place when he showed up behind her at noon. "Can I treat you to lunch?" He held up his well-worn cooler.

Climbing to her feet and stretching her sore back, she shook her head. "I can't eat your lunch, or you won't have enough energy for the rest of your work." She shot a glance at his sweaty hair. "And by the way, if you work as hard this afternoon as you did this morning, I'll see you at *my work* tonight."

"I'll be in labor and delivery? Now that's a trick."

"You know what I mean. You're pushing yourself so hard. I'm afraid you'll get hurt."

"Got a lot to do. We're way behind."

"You're not going to catch up by killing yourself."

His jaw tightened, but he relaxed it with obvious effort. "Will you share lunch with me or not? Don't worry about me starving. I always pack enough for an army, and then I eat like an army."

"I couldn't. Besides, I need to be getting back—"

"Here's a deal. I'll treat during my lunch hour, and you can treat me tonight on yours."

The heart drumming inside her chest made it hard to hold a nonchalant pose, but Charity gave it her best shot. How fortunate that she'd just set her trowel aside because it would have clanged to the ground, giving her away. Was he asking her out? She wasn't sure that anything in the West Oakland Regional Hospital cafeteria could qualify as date food, anyway. But it was the closest thing to a date she'd had in a long time.

When she finally peeked back at him, he stood watching her. The skin on her forearms tingled as if he'd touched her.

"Not a date or anything. Just trading lunches."

The tingling deserted her, and embarrassment quickly replaced it. Had he included that disclaimer for her benefit—or his? Either way, she was stuck. If she declined now, he would mistakenly assume she *wanted* to date him. If she agreed, she would have to confess something else to her mother…when she got around to doing it. Confessing won hands down as the lesser disaster.

"Sounds great. What's for lunch?"

"Sandwiches, veggies, fruit, a couple cookies and bottled water," he listed as he led her to the picnic table arranged under the lot's best shade tree.

"The last sounds the best. I'm dying of thirst."

Breaking the seal, he handed her the first plastic

bottle. "You mean you haven't had anything to drink all morning? And you're a nurse?"

Several swallows later she finally could answer him. "I just forgot to bring it. I usually remember."

He opened a second bottle, saluted her with it and took a long drink. "When you work outside all the time, you learn the hard way not to forget."

After spreading out the contents of his cooler on the table and handing her a turkey-and-lettuce sandwich, raw broccoli and an apple, he finally served himself.

"What a healthy lunch. Even on wheat bread." She took a big bite to show her appreciation.

"What were you expecting, bologna-on-white, cheesy curls and snack cakes?"

She chuckled. "Something like that."

"That used to be my daily menu. I still like white bread better. And I still think no sandwich is complete without cheese and mayonnaise. But I was a heart attack waiting to happen, and I was outgrowing my jeans, so I changed my ways."

She swallowed her bite of apple before answering. "It looks like you did a good job changing your diet."

"Still eat the cookies." He held up a sandwich bag with several chocolate chip cookies inside. "Try one. I made them myself."

"Wow, a jack-of-all-trades," she said, but accepted the treat he offered. "Hey, this is delicious." Licking her lips in appreciation, she accepted another.

"You sound surprised. You shouldn't be. I've had to take care of myself for a long time."

"Did your parents die when you were young?"

He jerked but eventually shook his head. "As far as I know, they're still alive. Somewhere."

"What do you mean? That they deserted you?"

Rick's chest tightened the way it did every time he revisited memories best forgotten. Why had he mentioned it? Hinted at it. Even knowing she would ask, he had started this. Nobody knew this stuff but Rusty and him, and he should have kept it that way.

But for a reason he didn't want to analyze, he started talking. "I was in kindergarten when the courts terminated their parental rights. I wasn't exactly in my parents' plans. The people who brought me into this world couldn't seem to get rid of me fast enough—or often enough.

"I'd been cared for by all of their friends and several strangers by the time a police officer found me baby-sitting myself for the weekend—at age five."

Charity gasped, her anguish visible, while he stored his own safely inside.

"Oh, Rick. That's horrible."

"It wasn't always bad. When I was lucky, I'd end up with Grandma. She always had hugs and cookies for me." The hugs were the only parts that mattered, but he didn't add that. "Other times I wasn't so lucky."

Charity's eyes shined with unspent tears on his behalf. Why did he suddenly feel like crying? He'd wept away that history behind closed doors decades ago.

Bringing it up again didn't help anyone. Him least of all.

"Did they hurt you?"

"No, I wasn't physically abused or anything. I was just an afterthought. Nobody really wanted me."

Why was he telling all this? Why couldn't he stop? She didn't need to hear his story of woe. But the way she leaned forward and tilted her head in a listening pose convinced him she wanted to.

"Your grandmother could have gotten custody of you."

His insides softened briefly with the few warm memories in a lifetime of cold ones. "She promised me we would live together—just us two. But one day she had a stroke, and the next day she was gone."

"Did you have to go to a foster home?"

"First one. Then another. Then another." When he finally chanced a look at her, he saw only pity in eyes. The last thing he needed or wanted was her feeling sorry for him. "But that's all water under the bridge. I don't have to rely on anybody but myself now, just the way I want it."

All nervous energy, he stuffed sandwich bags and napkins back in his cooler. No matter how hard he tried not to glance back at her, he couldn't prevent his gaze from being drawn there. But where he'd expected shock over his rude comment, he saw only acceptance in her small smile. He had no idea how to take that. At least she didn't ask anything further about his past. He didn't want to think about it, let alone talk anymore.

After he finished packing his things, he managed a polite goodbye before taking a few steps to the site.

"I guess I'll see you tonight," she called after him.

The folly of his earlier invitation stopped him where he stood. Who had come up with that hare-brained idea anyway? That the answer was obvious didn't make it any easier. Would going give her permission to needle more into his past? Well, he'd better get prepared because he couldn't back out now. With a deep breath, he faced her.

"Oh, yeah. When is your shift and when is your lunch? Are you working two to ten?"

She shook her head and grinned. "No, I'm on a twelve-hour shift tonight. Seven to seven." The last she said with a barely contained laugh.

"When does that place lunch?"

"At eleven. Or you can wait until my last break…at three o'clock."

He shook his head, the tension of the moment before evaporating as their natural camaraderie returned to its comfortable rhythm. The joking he could handle; the deep stuff was much harder. "No, I'll take the eleven. But you'd better feed me well."

"Oh, I promise."

Either her words or the way she emphasized just one—*promise*—compelled him to study her expression when good sense demanded he look away. Her impish smile confused him no less than his sudden urge to rush back to where she stood. What was wrong with him? He'd started making excuses to be near her. Did he keep seeking her out because he needed to be with someone or because he needed to be with *her?*

The thought chased him as he turned from her and crossed the yard, putting distance between them. Distance and time. He needed both if he planned to get his thoughts together before they met at eleven o'clock. He couldn't need her. He couldn't need anyone. Relying on people was too dangerous. Everyone he'd ever known—except God—had let him down, so why give someone else the chance to do it? Sure he was jaded, but it kept him safe.

As he fastened his tool belt around his hips for the second time that day, he could hear an engine purring to life behind him. But he wouldn't allow himself to glance back at Charity as she wheeled her car out of the drive. Not yet. Tonight would be soon enough.

Maybe after one more conversation with her, he could get her out of his system. Sure, she'd been nice to have around, a nice puzzle to contemplate as a diversion in his empty social life. But he shouldn't keep spending time with her. Confusing her. And himself. Even a patient with a cast-covered leg had to eventually heal and walk on his own. But was he ready to give up Charity Sims?

Chapter Eleven

You should have cancelled. The words she'd repeated in her mind all afternoon and evening skittered through her thoughts once more, adding mass to the already sizable knot in her gut. She should have called. She'd had plenty of time before work and even after her shift started nearly four hours before.

His business card, with his home and cellular phone numbers, lay crumpled and damp in one sweaty palm. She wiped the other one on the cotton pants of her scrubs. If only she'd left a message, then she wouldn't have been waiting in the empty cafeteria with dread for her early dinner guest.

Dread. A strong word for the jumble of emotions that also could be deemed anticipation. She fiddled with several cellophane-covered packages of vending machine food as guilt crowded her thoughts. It didn't matter that Rick hadn't called the meeting a date when she wished with all her heart that it were.

Rick isn't the man for you. She wondered how many times she'd have to tell herself that before she accepted it. What would Daddy say if he were alive? Mother had voiced her disapproval—loudly. One of the Ten Commandments demanded that she honor her father and mother. Could visiting with Rick be worth disobeying those hallowed rules? She'd promised herself she would tell her mother of her plan to target Rick with her mission work. But how soon? Did good intentions count when it came to sin?

"Where's lunch? I'm starved."

Rick's words startled her out of her anxious trance. He leaned against the doorway, sporting well-worn jeans and a chambray shirt. His shoulders appeared wider than she remembered, his waist narrower. Despite his fresh, clean-shaven appearance, only his strange expression caught her attention and held it. *And I thought I was nervous.*

"Great, because I've got the best *lunch* in town over here," she said, indicating the display on the table.

He cocked his head in doubt but strode toward her, anyway. A few feet from the table, he stopped short, laughter lighting his eyes.

"I'm missing my beauty sleep for this?" He pointed to the spread and yawned dramatically.

Charity glanced down at some cream-filled cakes with a shelf life longer than the national average for humans. "Did I mention the cafeteria hot kitchen closes after eight?"

Rolling his eyes, he tapped an index finger against

his lips to appear deep in thought. "No," he said with an exaggerated shake of his head. "I don't believe you did."

"Oh…sorry." She paused, trying to contain her mirth. "The cafeteria closes after eight."

"Thanks for the tip." Laughter lit his eyes, but he didn't crack a smile.

"Don't let the packaging fool you. This is gourmet stuff."

Pulling her best game show hostess imitation, she waved her hand to show off the display. "There are four sandwiches, and only one of them has Sandwich Spread on the label. What do you think is in that?"

"I don't even want to know."

"And look at these snack crackers." She pointed to the package of sandy-colored ones. "They come with a cheese filling instead of the traditional peanut butter."

"That is amazing."

When Rick leaned in for a closer look, Charity caught a whiff of his outside-fresh soap and spicy cologne. Awareness settled over them like a fine mist, silencing background noises and focusing the ultra-violet lights on just one table. She met his gaze and didn't look away when she should have. Her mouth dry, she didn't speak. Besides, if she had, she probably would have slipped and said something about how he smelled as good as the great outdoors.

Rick dropped into the seat across from her, not showing any residual shock from the current that had just passed between them. "Okay, let's eat."

Grateful for something to make her stop wringing her hands, Charity divvied up the vending machine spoils. "One for you and one for me. One for you and one for—"

He held up hand to halt her just as she was about to slide the sandwich-spread sandwich in front of him. "Oh, no, no. I couldn't possibly take that specialty from you. It's all yours."

"No, you're the guest. I insist."

He crossed his index fingers in front of him in an *X*. "That thing should have a skull and crossbones on the label. Better look. It just might."

Laughter that started deep in her lungs burst forth in a gasp. He laughed with her, the corners of his eyes crinkling and his baritone melody filling the cafeteria with its richness.

"Okay, okay. Neither of us will take that one." She pushed it to the far side of the table.

"Hey, this is pretty good," Rick said, after swallowing the first bite of chicken salad.

She took a big bite of tuna salad. "You see, I said it was gourmet."

"Guess I learned my lesson."

"You sure did."

"Hey, pass some of those sandwich crackers over here."

After she tossed him a bag, they munched quietly a few minutes. As long as she could remember, she'd wished for someone to be with her this way. To talk or not to talk. And it was great having Rick for a friend. Still, she wondered if their friendship would be enough to fill that empty space inside her.

"Does your mom meet you here for lunch on your night shifts?" Rick asked, his tone overly casual.

"Sometimes," she answered, her comfort from a few seconds before drifting away.

He met her gaze. "You told her not to come tonight, didn't you?" Without waiting for an answer, he continued. "She doesn't like me much."

"She likes you fine." That he wasn't buying it couldn't have been more obvious in the way he lifted an eyebrow, letting the same side of his mouth follow in a half grin. "Okay, you're not at the top of her list."

"Close to the bottom, I'd say."

What could she say to that? She took her time coming up with something while chewing on her last bite of snack cake. "You know how parents are."

"Can't say that I do."

She groaned inside. Of course he couldn't know about his parents, and she could offer no excuse for hers. His grimace matched the expression she was holding inside. He'd called his past "water under the bridge," but it kept trickling back into the present. If she helped him deal with the pain of his parents' desertion, then maybe he could put it to rest.

"Why weren't you ever adopted?" *Way to go. A really great starting question.* She waited for him to push his chair back and give her a nice view of his back as he left the building. But he only sat looking past at some point on the muted-pattern wallpaper.

"The courts had adoption in mind when they made me a ward of the state. Ten foster homes later... Well, that's how it goes."

"Weren't any of your foster parents good to you? Didn't they care?"

"They probably all did. They tried to get close to me, I guess, but I wanted distance. Demanded it."

An urgency to touch him, to connect somehow, became so overwhelming that she gripped her hands in her lap to hold back. In the hard lines of his masculine face, she saw a small boy's image, a child who didn't know how to reach out. The man still couldn't.

"Did you get into trouble?"

"Only whenever possible," he said, setting aside his snack cake. He flashed her a close-up glimpse of the scars on his hands and knuckles. "Every new home meant different schools. Always the new kid."

"I bet those hurt," she said of the visible scars and those that extended under the rolled sleeves of his shirt and farther still beneath his battle thickened skin.

As if he recognized the hidden meaning in her comment, he met her gaze for a fraction of a second before glancing at his watch. When he looked up again, he touched the bridge of his nose with his index finger. "Hey, did you notice this?"

"Broken nose?"

"Just twice. Cut once." He pointed to a small scar.

"Did you ever get in trouble with the law?"

He shook his head no. "I don't know why, either. I probably became a troublemaker in the first place because everyone expected I would. But as I got older, I just kept to myself, spending all my time in wood shop class. I surprised everyone by being good at that.''

His last statement gripped her insides in an unrelenting fist. No wonder he pushed himself so hard. Everyone he knew had expected him to fail. He probably still believed some of their negative messages.

''They were wrong, you know.''

His eyes widened. ''What do you mean? I don't blame any of my foster parents. They tried their best.''

''Did you ever have a girlfriend?'' Her ill-timed question surprised her no less than her hope that his answer would be yes. She was tempted to be jealous, but she desperately needed to hear that someone— anyone—had loved Rick and made him feel loved.

But he only stared at her several seconds and shook his head. ''A few. Nothing serious. What about you?''

''The same.'' She forced a smile to her lips for both of their sakes.

''Do you want to get married and have kids someday?''

Charity swallowed hard, a knot forming in her throat. Could he understand what it felt like to dream and to watch hope slip away with every added birthday candle?

''Sure, I do,'' she finally choked out, tilting her head to turn the question back to him.

He shrugged. ''I've never really thought about it.''

''Really?'' She almost laughed at that, but she

wasn't about to admit she'd thought of little else for years.

"Whoever he is, he'll be a lucky guy," Rick said but didn't look at her.

Surprise and pleasure entwined to warm Charity. It was the nicest thing he'd ever said to her. Briefly, she wondered what her future would be like with Rick in it. She shifted in her chair, needing to escape the intensity of their conversation.

Still, a question burned inside her until she felt forced to ask, "Have you told anyone else about your past?"

Rick glanced at the wall clock and then started gathering the plastic wrappers. "Just Rusty."

Confusion tempered her pleasure at being welcomed into his confidence. His openness was so contradictory to her earlier perception of him. On just how many counts could she have been wrong about him?

Again, the image of Rick as a neglected child slipped into her thoughts, wrapping itself like a tourniquet around her heart. But it didn't stop the bleeding. She felt his pain so intensely that she could almost see his scars on her own knuckles, inside her soul. The responsibility of his trust was a heavy burden. Could she withstand the weight? Was she worthy of his belief in her?

Dear God, please show me what you want me to do, she prayed. But the answer didn't come as instantly as she'd hoped, remaining as elusive as her confidence in her faith. For so long she had dreamed of developing a deep connection with a man, where her emotions would be but an extension of his. She felt that connection with Rick, her friend. It should have amazed her, exhilarated her. Instead, it scared her to death.

"See you soon," Rick called after Charity as she hurried back to work. But he had to tamp back the pleasure produced by the prospect of seeing her again. A sinking feeling in his gut rooted him firmly to the chair. Why had he opened to her in the first place, and why did he continue to gut himself every time he came near her? *You never take chances like that.* So why was he reaching out to her for a connection he didn't need? And shouldn't want.

He no longer even asked himself, why Charity? The warm, caring side of her personality that she displayed with increasing frequency, and her compassion for him and for others, drew him to her. His conviction that he needed to help her escape the heavy hand of her controlling mother pulled him even more.

Concerning her relationship with the Lord, she seemed to be missing something he'd found. He wanted that peace for her, as well. God had accepted him, warts and all. If only Charity knew the Father would do the same for her.

"You being selfless? You're lying to yourself." Rick glanced nervously about the empty room, realizing he'd spoken aloud. That was the most honest thought he'd had since she'd left the room. Not that he didn't want good things for her, especially a solid relationship with God, but he kidded himself to believe he didn't want more.

Whoever she chooses, he'll be a lucky guy. That was as ridiculous as it sounded. He didn't want some *lucky guy* to have her. Unless he was the one.

A collection of still shots flashed before him as he pushed himself up from the chair and collected the last pile of plastic wrappers. Charity pointing her finger in condemnation, wielding Scripture as a weapon. Then Charity rolling her eyes, her low laugh filtering straight from her lungs into his. On another occasion, her eyes brimming with tears, as she listened to his history…and cared.

When had he glossed over the earlier images of her to cherish the latter? When had his heart forgotten all the reasons not to care for her? *The only times you've felt anything close to peace lately were when she was with you. Big admission for a confirmed loner.* The reality of it terrified him, but it didn't stop him from wishing. Just when he should have raced in the opposite direction, he found he didn't want to take a step.

Frustration over his lack of self-preservation stayed with him, even after he returned to Milford. Being honest with himself had always been dangerous. Now it seemed downright suicidal.

Rick pulled into the garage just off the alley and tromped up the back walk. His house had never looked so empty before. He yawned as he unlocked the back door. Good thing he hadn't agreed to meet her at three o'clock.

As he mounted the stairs and climbed in bed, he replayed their conversation in his memory. How strange that he'd cut himself open and poured out his deepest secrets, but she'd barely bled a drop. "That's not fair," he muttered.

It was about time he had an invitation into Charity's psyche. Sure, he knew what her mother had programmed her to expect out of life, but what did she want for herself? In her heart of hearts where no one could watch or censor, did she have dreams for something more?

Suddenly, he needed to know everything about her. Even the things she wasn't ready to acknowledge about herself. Curiosity…that was why he would phone her tomorrow—make that later today. To ask her questions about her life. *And for a date,* his subconscious added without permission.

Rick sighed and pulled the sheets over him. He was tired. Of constantly trying to prove he was worth something. Of lying to himself.

Father, lead me in the way You would have me go. Please make it clear to me if Charity is the choice You have for me.

With that, he turned and buried his face into the pillow, convinced he would find some peace in sleep. He would call Charity later for no other reason than he wanted to be with her. And he wanted to date her. He closed his eyes, certain he would carry thoughts of her into his dreams.

* * *

Charity awoke Tuesday afternoon, rested for the first time in days. A glance at the clock told her why. At nearly four o'clock, she'd slept a good six hours. Since she expected her mom home by five, she wasn't surprised to hear the phone ring. Maybe Mother would bring home roasted chicken for dinner. She was starved.

A smile still on her lips at the memory of her last interesting meal, she lifted the receiver.

"Hello, Mother," she said in a sleep-roughened voice.

"Hello, Sleeping Beauty. Sorry. Not your mother."

Like she hadn't already figured that out and her face wasn't already tingling from just below her eyebrows to her collarbones. *Sleeping Beauty?*

"Hey, Rick." She crossed her arms over her jersey nightgown although he couldn't see her. "What's up?"

"Did you spend the day dreaming? You just woke up, didn't you?"

Charity swallowed hard. *Relax. Those were just casual questions.* He couldn't possibly know about that hand-holding dream nor that cliché scene where she'd run through a wheat field with her arms outstretched…to him. She planned to keep her secret, too.

"I don't even know if I'm awake yet," she said, sidestepping the dream question altogether.

"Hey, lucky you. Morning came awfully early for me after last night."

Last night. If she hadn't agreed to that payback lunch, then she wouldn't have been so confused today. "Remember, I didn't get off work until seven this morning."

"Oh, that's right. Glad you got some rest."

His conversation confused her as much as her dreams had. Why did she continue to think of Rick in impossible terms? He would never be an appropriate choice for her, would never fulfill her mother's expectations. Or hers, of course. "Hey, thanks for calling, but I was about to step into the shower, so—"

"You missed a beautiful day while you were sleeping," he interrupted her, his voice breaking up on the cell phone.

"I'm sorry I missed it, but—"

"Did you notice that the red oak on the church's front lawn is starting to turn?"

His strange words took her aback. In fact, this whole conversation was surreal. "That one is always beautiful in the fall."

"Just the slightest bit of crimson on the leaves at the very top, the ones closest to Heaven," he said.

She couldn't help smiling into the receiver over a guy who noticed fall colors and thought of trees as reaching up to God. She found herself as reluctant as he seemed to be to end the call. "So...how was work?"

"Busy."

Charity scrambled for something to fill the pause, but *I had a great time last night* just wouldn't do.

"I was thinking," Rick said finally. "There's a

comedy playing at the Milford Cinema. I thought we could catch a flick and maybe grab a bite later.''

The way her pulse tripped and her palms dampened convinced Charity she'd heard him right. He'd just asked her out on a real date. She felt as if she'd waited a lifetime for him to ask and, at the same time, wished he hadn't invited her. It only made her want something she had no business wishing for, had no right dreaming about.

''You mean a date? Maybe that's not such—''

''Sure, a date, but not a serious one. Come on. We'll have fun. We always have fun together.''

He was right about that much. The best times she could think of lately were spent in his company. But that fact couldn't be enough. Not when he'd changed the rules in their relationship by using the word *date*. She had to do the right thing. ''You know—''

''Come on. I need you. If you don't go, I'll be forced to go to the movies alone.''

At what moment she lost her battle, she wasn't sure, but the white flag in her mind told her the bad news. How could she refuse him when she knew, despite his plea in jest, that he really might need her? Later, she would worry about telling her mother the whole story.

''When you put it that way…okay,'' she said ''How about I meet you at the cinema? What time did you say the movie started?''

She stepped to the table and readied a pen and paper to take down the information, but he didn't say anything. ''Rick, are you still there?''

"Yeah."

"I asked what time the show is so I can meet you—"

"Charity, I don't think that's going to work."

"What do you mean?" Anxiety slashed through her, with dread flitting at the edges of her consciousness. Had he changed his mind? If only she'd said no in the first place to protect her fragile heart. "What won't work?"

"The movie's at five-forty-five, but we agreed it was a date, right?"

She cleared her throat. "Right."

"Well, I have a policy about picking up all of my *dates* at their houses. Will your mother be home by then?" This time he didn't wait for her response. "It will be great seeing her again."

Charity's pulse pounded an erratic rhythm at her temple. Her shoulders felt pressed against a wall although she stood in the middle of the living room. Rick was forcing her to choose. To be with him, she would have to acknowledge their seedling of a relationship to her mother. No more subterfuge.

"Rick, maybe we shouldn't do this after all."

For the longest time, he said nothing, but when he finally did, he lowered his voice. "Do you want to go out with me or not?" He paused, the line empty except for cell phone static. "Because I want to be with you."

Charity stared at the receiver, the dark plastic handset shaking in her trembling hand. He'd said more than he just wanted to go out with her. He wanted to *be* with her, and if she were honest with herself, she'd admit she needed him, too.

Rick cleared his throat. "Do you or don't you?"

She sucked a breath in, holding on to it and the last safety net her fear provided. And then she released both.

"Yes, I do."

"Good," Rick said with what sounded like a rush of air. "Then it's settled. We're both adults. I just can't be your secret behind your mother's back. Either we go out with her knowledge, or we should forget the whole idea. What do you say?"

Charity dug her teeth into her lip, finding resolve she hadn't been aware she possessed. "Pick me up at quarter after five."

Chapter Twelve

"You're doing *what?*"

Each of Laura's syllables increased about an octave, until the third word became a shriek. As much as Charity expected a negative reaction, the volume shook her. She should have waited a few more minutes after her mother arrived home from work to announce her plans. But that only would have delayed the yelling.

Charity straightened her shoulders and faced her seething mother. The secret was out now. She couldn't—no, wouldn't—go back.

"I said I'm going to the movies and dinner with Rick McKinley. He'll be here in about ten minutes." Steadying her nervous hands, she glanced out the window, hoping he wouldn't be early.

"Then you'd better call him before he leaves home because you're not going."

The calming breath Charity had inhaled choked her

instead. She faced the wall mirror, fiddling with her peach sweater set and stuffing her fists in her jeans pockets.

"Mother, I'm going."

"Then I've failed as your mother." Laura stood behind her daughter, joining their reflections in the mirror. She hung her head in a sympathy-generating pose. "If I haven't taught you about being unequally yoked with an unbeliever, then I haven't taught you anything."

Charity faced Laura and waited for remorse to overtake her, but she only ended up feeling annoyed. Had it always been so easy for her mother to play on her emotions? Her resentment was new and a bit disconcerting, but she focused on it to keep her resolve. "It's just a movie and dinner. Rick didn't ask me to get a marriage license. I'm probably safe for at least the next few hours."

Instead of furious, Laura appeared sad. "You're not safe. Your heart…least of all." She lowered her gaze.

Her heart? Did Mother know something about heartbreak herself? The questions Rick had asked her about her parents' relationship repeated in Charity's mind. Did she really know if they'd been happy? "What are you saying?"

When Laura looked up again, she had pasted that pursed-lips expression of disappointment firmly back in place. "I'm saying that I forbid you to go out with Mr. McKinley. As long as you live under my roof, you will obey my rules, and those rules include not dating an unbeliever.''

A ringing began in Charity's ears and climbed out to claim the rest of her. How could her mother be so judgmental, so closed-minded? Charity couldn't remember ever having been so angry with Laura before.

Forcing her voice to remain steady, she finally answered. ''Mother, I'd like to remind you that I pay half the bills here. Besides that, I became an adult more than a decade ago.''

Laura's face flushed crimson as she crossed her arms over her chest. ''I cannot believe your belligerence. What has this…man…done to you?''

''Rick hasn't done anything to me besides be my friend. And for your information, he is just as much a believer as you are. It's presumptuous of you to judge his heart.''

Hadn't Charity been just as quick to jump to conclusions when she'd met Rick? Now she was almost jealous of the confidence he had in his faith. Would she ever know that kind of peace?

''Me, judging? Well, if I am, I know one young lady who isn't honoring her mother right now.''

Charity fisted her hands at her sides, her nails pressing into her palms until they hurt. ''Oh, I'm honoring you, Mother, by not telling you what I really think.''

''And I'm going to honor *you* by not being present to tell your Mr. McKinley what *I* think.'' With that, she marched off to her bedroom, slamming the door behind her.

Charity jerked at the fury-filled bang, alienation draining her excitement as much as her resolve. Was one date really worth estranging the mother who had always loved her? A stab at independence couldn't be worth the pain it had already caused.

Honor your father and mother. Those words struck her with fresh blows. But hadn't she been trying to do that all her life? She'd been a good daughter. Until now.

"Okay, I won't go." Her words barely beat a whisper, but still she sneaked a glimpse up the empty staircase to see if her mother had overheard. Her admission filled her with defeat. Taking the easy way out had become a career for her. Breaking out of that mold was too hard, its ramifications too painful.

The truck's rumble in the drive yanked her away from those heavy thoughts. With a trembling hand, she pulled back a corner of the curtain.

"I'm sorry. Thank you for the offer, but I've changed my mind," she practiced, still at a whisper. Would Rick hear the yearning she couldn't extract from her voice?

At the top of the stairs, the door to her mother's room cracked open. Charity and Rick would have an audience when they finally faced each other. When he continued sitting behind the wheel as seconds ticked by, she wondered if he wanted to delay that meeting as much as she did.

At last, the truck door swung wide, and he stepped out, strutting up the drive with a determined pace so unlike his usual saunter. Charity tried to still the mass of butterflies fluttering beneath her rib cage. Then he glanced at the corner of the window from which she viewed him. His gaze seemed to penetrate the heavy brocade drapes. So like the way he'd always seen through her.

The words of her practiced speech dissolved with each step he took closer. Before he made it up on the porch, she had her hand on the doorknob. Moving forward felt like cliff diving, but there was something liberating about a free fall into the unknown. Yanking the door open, she took that first terrifying leap.

Rick raised his hand to knock, ignoring the suspicion that he'd made a mistake in coming. But the door flew open before his hand connected with the rich wood.

"It's you, Rick."

She said it as if he were valuable, not the jerk who'd challenged her allegiance to her mother for his selfish curiosity. When earlier it had felt heroic to make her see how her mother controlled her, now his actions only seemed cruel.

"Expecting someone else?"

He wished *he* were someone else. Then he might deserve her. She was sweet and funny. Compassionate. Brilliant.

Can you stop already? He breathed deeply. How long had he stood there, staring at her like an idiot?

She drew her eyebrows together, appearing confused. "No, you'd be the one."

The one. He'd never be the man she wanted, the

person she'd been trained to expect. Though he'd known it all along, only now did that reality fill him with hopelessness. "Good, then can I come in?"

Charity glanced nervously over her shoulder but backed away from the door. The living room he entered was as empty and as overly formal as the last time he'd visited.

"I thought I'd get the chance to see your mother again before we left?" *Shooing me off the porch with a broom.* "Where is she?"

Charity's glance toward the stairs provided a clue. "Mother needed…to be in her room right now."

"Did she develop this need before or after you told her we were going out together?"

She chewed her bottom lip but met his gaze. "After."

"You're sure? You really told her?"

"Rick—" she paused until he looked at her "—I told her." Charity pointed to the stairs and then to her ear, signaling him that Laura was listening.

His mouth dried at the thought of the sacrifice Charity had made for him. "It would have been great to see your mother," he said for the benefit of both Sims women. "Oh, well. Next time. We'd better get going, or we'll be late for the movie."

Charity glanced at the stairs again and paused so long that Rick wondered if she'd changed her mind. Anxiety gripped him with frigid fingers. He'd almost driven away himself, and yet the thought of her canceling left him feeling alone before she could take a step away from him. But then she faced him and pressed her shoulders back.

"I'll grab my jacket."

"That movie was great. I don't remember ever laughing so hard," Charity said a few hours later as she and Rick walked along Main Street, past the new shopping plaza. She also couldn't remember the hairs on her arms under her sweater ever feeling so electric without static, but she didn't mention that.

"I thought the funniest scene was when soda came out your nose." He leaned closer until they bumped shoulders.

She stuck out her tongue at him but ended up laughing anyway. Could this night have been more perfect? Not a cloud marred the smooth blanket of sky that had darkened in minutes to navy blue. Already a sprinkling of the first stars studded the cloth. These natural night-lights brought a shiny glow to storefront windows they passed, continuing farther south.

What were we talking about? Oh, the soda thing. Her nose still burned from that. Though it seemed too late to respond to his comment, she said, "No funnier than when you dumped the whole tub of popcorn on the floor."

"Hey, that popcorn cost me nearly all my life savings. I thought about scooping it off the floor."

"The only reason you didn't was because I grabbed your arm." It hadn't been much of a sacrifice to touch him. Every brush of his hand, every whiff of his woodsy aftershave, had been pleasant interruptions during the show.

"I recognize that place." Rick pointed across the street to the gazebo from a few days before, and their gazes met and held.

She stared at the structure she would never see the same now. Neither spoke for a long time, but Charity didn't mind, their simple closeness making her warm despite the dipping temperatures. Rick seemed to enjoy just being with her. What she said appeared to interest him. All her life she'd been waiting for someone to listen to her, and he not only listened but he really heard.

Later—much later—she would acknowledge what a mistake it had been to come, but for now, she felt only pure delight.

Mother was likely still home brooding, preparing to give Charity a huge lecture. Later. She'd think about that later. Now she was having the time of her life.

"A penny for your thoughts." Rick spoke so softly that he only splintered the silence rather than fracturing it. Yet his strange expression sent her thoughts racing. How long had he been watching her and wondering how far away she'd traveled?

"We're both kind of quiet tonight." She only wished she had a funny joke for him, something that would send their conversation back to comfortable territory. Her nerves were on alert, making it impossible to think clearly.

Then Rick reached for her hand, and she could focus only on that point of contact. As unsure as she'd been of everything else in her life, his touch felt amazingly right. She shivered, the tremble reaching her fingertips and probably filtering into his.

Rick slowed. "Are you cold?"

She could only shake her head. It was impossible to sense temperature when her very discrimination of time and place had collapsed. She could be anywhere at all—in cold or heat, in safety or danger—and nothing would matter except being there with Rick.

"Here we are." He stopped in front of her favorite restaurant, Appeteaser. When he released her hand to open the door, Charity chilled at the loss of his touch.

Soft lighting and soothing music greeted them inside, creating a romantic setting so unnecessary in an evening that had already taken on a fairy-tale light. The clink of water glasses and the sound of muffled voices only added to the atmosphere.

"…sounds good."

Charity startled at his words, realizing she hadn't been listening again. Rick pointed to the list of the evening's specials written in script on a decorative chalkboard. Funny, she'd been hungry earlier. Once more she looked out into the lemon-lit room, where shadows shimmied across guests' faces, and she turned back to him.

"Would you mind if we skipped dinner? After all that popcorn…"

"Yeah, I'm not hungry, either."

He kindly neglected to mention that he'd spilled

most of the popcorn, so neither had eaten much. "I'll take you home."

"Is that what you want?"

Surprise registered in his eyes, and his Adam's apple jerked. "No."

Charity couldn't begin to describe the confusion and trepidation volleying for control inside her. But when she met Rick's gaze, both settled in a calm sea.

"Do you want to go for a walk?" she said, zipping her jacket over her cardigan. "We could go to the park."

He held out his arm. Her hand fit naturally in his, their fingers curling together so easily. The notion struck her that she never wanted him to release his gentle hold on her hand—or her heart. Although she tucked the thought in the back of her mind where it belonged, she squeezed his hand tighter as they stepped back outside. How warm her heart felt when he squeezed back.

Even if this were a Cinderella kind of night where she would awaken to the ashes and soot of her regular life, she would not deny herself the joy of it, just this once.

"Don't you think it's too cold for the park?" Rick stopped and released her hand to snap his jacket.

"Not too cold for me." With a grin, she jogged ahead, turning only long enough to wave with a sweeping gesture for him to follow. "It's a great night."

Rick was certain she was right about that. *It's too right. Too great. And too dangerous.* Though he hated feeling vulnerable, he couldn't turn back now. He didn't even want to.

"Hey, wait up," he said, picking up his step. In front of the sub shop that looked like a converted train car, he caught up with her, tucking her hand through the bend in his arm.

The world felt right again as he touched her, when it had seemed so wrong while she'd been out of reach. He didn't want to analyze his feelings. For once, he just wanted to enjoy.

"Should we risk it?" she indicated the narrow train trestle that scared everyone enough in daylight, let alone with darkness enclosing Milford in its shadowy cocoon.

Why not? I'm risking everything else. "Let's do it." But first he touched his index finger to his lips to indicate they should be quiet. "Do you hear any cars?"

She shook her head.

"Okay, on three. One, two, three." He grabbed her hand and raced with her through the short tunnel.

Emerging on the other side, they saw a pair of headlights still five hundred feet up the road.

"Whew!" Charity whooped as they dodged to the roadside.

He should have released her once they reached the entrance to the park, but he couldn't let go. It felt too right. He stopped past the park sign and tried to inhale a breath, his lungs tight.

"This must be what you call 'extreme dating,'" Charity said, her breath melding with the heavy, cold air. "What do we do next time, skydiving or bungee jumping?"

"I was thinking more of a quick hike up Everest and then some snorkeling off the Great Barrier Reef."

"It's a date."

They both laughed, but Rick sensed tension building between them. Charity's grasp on his hand loosened. Would there ever be another date? If he had any sense, he'd make sure there was no repeat to a night like this. The stars already shone too brightly. The air smelled too crisp.

If all these things weren't flashing enough warning lights, the warmth that seeped from her fingertips into his very soul provided an outright siren.

Charity tugged her hand free and dashed toward the fenced-in playground known as the Riverbend Playscape. "Bet I can swing higher than you."

"I wouldn't have thought you were the betting kind," he called but chased her toward the swings, crossing a carpet of wood chips. She'd already established her lead in the race toward the sky by the time he hopped into the swing beside her.

"You know what I meant," she said, swishing past. "It's a challenge."

"Oh…a challenge." Never able to resist one of those, he pumped and stretched his legs, sending the chilly wind swirling around him. But he sensed the weightlessness inside his stomach had less to do with swinging and more to do with a life out of control.

"I win. I win." Charity sounded breathless as she declared victory from her summit.

"Do over," he called out, unable to keep the laughter from his voice.

She coasted to a stop, dragging her feet over the spongy safety surfacing under the swing. "You're a bad sport, aren't you?"

"For your information, I'm an excellent sport. I just think if there was a line judge, you would be called out."

"Oh, yeah?"

"Yeah."

"Let's settle it then. Race me to the park shelter. Ready, set, go." With that she jumped from the swing and sprinted through the playground entrance, taking advantage of another head start.

Rick hopped down, already in motion, as he followed her through the yellow park-light haze. She ran without looking back, her loose hair chasing after her in a golden stream. His chest burned and his limbs ached from exertion as he clamored across the shelter floor.

"Tilt. Offside. Foul. Flag on the play," he called out between gasps.

"Quit your whining. I'm enjoying my victory." She didn't even look winded, and he was about to burst a lung.

"A cheater's victory," he finally managed.

"Are you calling me a cheater?"

"If it walks like a duck and it talks like a duck, then guess what? Quack. Quack."

"Well, I might be a duck, but this duck is faster than you and I can prove it." She hopped off the table top to the bench and then onto the floor, poised to sprint away.

Something crazy inside him compelled him to close his fingers over her wrist before she could run away again. Symbolic, perhaps, but he couldn't stand the thought of her leaving him. He didn't know when he'd first put his heart at risk, but this sinking ship was taking on more water by the minute, and he couldn't stop it. Worse yet, he had no desire to cling to the last shreds of his good sense.

With the smallest tug on her wrist, Rick brought her back toward him. Visible in the soft light that flooded into the east side of the structure, Charity stood rod straight. She looked so sweet, so unsure. A need to protect her clutched him, its fierceness startling.

"Don't run. I can't handle another race," he said, still cradling her wrist between his thumb and forefinger. Her skin warmed his hand, and her pulse drummed steadily against his fingertips.

"I can't run, either. I'm beat." She glanced at the line of trees that hid the Huron River just beyond.

"Yeah, me, too."

They weren't talking about running through the park anymore, and she had to know it as much as he did. He was tired of running. So tired. He had no energy left to convince himself he was this "island" poet John Donne swore no man could be. That he needed no one but himself.

He did need. He needed her.

The night grew silent except for the soft rumble of

the occasional car traveling along Main Street or turning on Canal Street. He either heard or felt her exhalation, their faces close enough to share the cool night air.

Rick stared at her mouth, knowing he shouldn't kiss her but just as aware he would. He needed to connect with her, to draw her into the circle of his arms and touch her heart as deeply as she'd touched his. When like had become love, he didn't know, but it had transformed as surely as his heart had changed when he'd met God face-to-face.

Still, as he stared into her lovely face, he found it easier to waver on the precipice than to leap. So he waited a little longer. As if she recognized his internal battle, Charity stared at him in wide-eyed uneasiness. Her vulnerability pushed him over the edge.

Releasing her wrist, he rested his hands gently just behind her elbows, drawing her to him. When only a breath separated them, Rick stopped. "I'd really like to kiss you, Charity. May I?"

She drew in a breath and held it before letting her exhalation become words. "I'd like that."

Rick leaned in, intent on touching her first, but Charity lifted up then, beginning that wondrous first kiss with a bump of lips and a clink of front teeth. Yanking back, she pressed her fist to her probably bruised mouth, struggling to contain a nervous titter. Unable to resist, he joined her, snickering before laughing out loud.

Then he did the most natural thing he could imagine by closing his arms around her and burying his hands in her silky hair. How perfectly she fit there with her head resting on his shoulder.

"Now that was fun," he said when he finally pulled her away from him and gazed into her shadowed face. "Do you want to try that again?" He waited for her nod before continuing. "Okay, you stay still. Let me do the work."

He lowered his head and pressed his lips to hers. This sweetest, gentlest kiss of his lifetime captured his breath. It didn't feel like a kiss at all…but a promise. The intensity of it scared him enough to withdraw.

But she smiled at him, melting his attempt to freeze his heart. He lowered his head for a second caress, sweeter than the first though he wouldn't have thought it possible. Never wanting to pull away again, he slanted his mouth across hers and deepened the kiss. She surprised and pleased him by responding.

He tamped back the masculine satisfaction that came with claiming her as his own, though at that moment he could think of nothing more perfect. But as he opened his eyes in time to see her lids flutter and lift, he saw the same trust and hope he'd begun to feel in his own soul. How humbling it was to confess that his heart had already been claimed.

Chapter Thirteen

The wave of elation Charity had ridden on during the long walk back to Rick's truck turned to low tide as they drove up to her house. The cut of the ignition signaled Rick's time to leave her, and the thought of that separation caused a void to form deep inside her.

"Thank you so much for tonight. I had a lot of fun. The movie was great." Her words sounded rushed in her ears, but she couldn't stop their flow as she gripped the door handle.

Nervousness that had evaporated while she'd rested in his arms reappeared with force now that she'd returned to her mother's house and her own real world. She needed to face the consequences of her choices, no matter how much she wanted to stay here with Rick.

"I'd better get inside. Thanks again...." She let her words fall away as she lifted the door handle, sending light flooding into the truck cab.

But Rick laid his hand on her arm. "Charity, wait."

Déjà vu swirled around her with the memory of that long-ago car ride, when Andrew had gently put her aside. Rick's grasp on her arm and his words were just like the youth minister's. Would his message be the same? Would he push her away as Andrew had? No, she would die if he did that. With dread, she turned back to him.

But Rick only touched his thumb and forefinger beneath her chin and tilted her face upward for a feathery kiss, a tiny reminder of their tender exchange at the park. Too soon it had ended, but she felt his closeness all the same. As if he'd promised to stay by her.

"We'd better go up."

"We?" She looked up to where the porch light burned. "Don't worry. I'll be fine. I'll just let myself in."

"Excuse me." He paused until she looked back at him. "I have a rule about always walking my *dates* to the door."

Despite her anxiety, she grinned. "You sure have a lot of rules about dating."

"You're about to learn every one," he said before climbing out and crossing to help her out of the truck.

Every one. How peaceful his words made her feel. There would be more to their relationship than just this Cinderella night. And she was ready to trade those glass slippers for the superior reality of being with him.

When he rested his hand behind her elbow, she leaned into his comfort as they approached the front door. She could never remember feeling so safe, so protected.

They'd reached the first step when Laura stomped out the front door. "So you're finally coming in. No daughter of mine will be parking in cars."

Charity's cheeks burned. "Mother, how could you?"

"How could I? How could *I!*" Laura took a deep breath, obviously trying to regain control of her emotions. When she spoke again, her voice still sounded strained. "How could *you* betray *me* by dating this…this…man?"

A pulse pounded in Charity's ears as fury overwhelmed her, constricting her throat. Rick rubbed his thumb against her elbow to show his support, but still her thoughts raced.

"Betray *you?* Mother, this isn't about *you* at all. It's about Rick and me. It was only a date." She couldn't find a way to express what an understatement that was, but the squeeze of her heart confirmed it.

"I forbade you to go out with this…unbeliever." She finally glanced at Rick but only glared at him. "You ignored my wishes. I don't know what he's done to you, but…"

Laura's words fell away as Rick stepped forward and became a human barricade between Charity and her mother. "Mrs. Sims, believe whatever you choose to about me. Only God's opinion about my heart matters, anyway. But aren't you arguing a moot point?

We already went out.'' He glanced back at Charity over his shoulder. ''Your daughter has made her choice.''

Charity moved around him until she stood at his side, trembling inside far more over Rick's chivalrous actions than her mother's anger. Had anyone taken her side before? She'd always wondered what it felt like to be cherished. Now she knew, and she couldn't have felt less worthy.

''Aren't you going to say something to him?'' Laura's voice sounded shrill, but she wore a placid expression.

Obviously, Laura expected her daughter to refute Rick's comment. Charity just couldn't do it. She was sick of lying, especially to herself. But, as instructed, she turned to the man who had so recently held her in his arms. ''Rick, I need to talk with Mother alone. Do you mind?''

''Of course not.'' He reached for her hand, curling his fingers over hers in a protective hold. ''Are you sure you'll be okay? I'll stay if you need me.''

''I'll be fine.''

Rick pressed a kiss to Charity's knuckles. ''Then I'll call you tomorrow. I had a great time tonight, and I can't wait to take you out again.'' Turning to Laura, he said, ''Good night, Mrs. Sims.''

Laura didn't answer, but Rick didn't seem to expect it. He didn't glance back as he strode to his truck, climbed in and backed down the driveway. As soon his car reached the street, Charity entered the house, her mother close at her heels.

"You won't see that man again—not if I have anything to say about it," Laura said as she pushed the heavy door closed behind her.

"That's just it, Mother. You *don't* have anything to say about it."

"How dare you talk to me like that!" Laura planted her hands on her hips and stepped so close that each of her words came with bursts of air against Charity's cheek. "You have no right—"

"But I do have rights. It's my decision what I do with my life. Even who I choose to date." Charity took the same hard stance as her mother. "I just didn't realize it until recently."

With stiff steps, Laura moved across the living room. "Until that awful man invaded our lives."

Charity followed her, teeth clenched. When her mother turned to face her, she had to shove back the fury threatening to overtake her. She couldn't lose control now. This conversation was long overdue. "Can you hear yourself? You're upset because I met Rick, and he convinced me I had the right to make my own decisions? Are you angry that I've stopped being your puppet?"

Laura shook her head slowly. "You're such a disappointment. I'm so glad your father isn't here to see the disrespectful daughter you've become."

Charity's determination trembled as much as her shoulders. Could she bear to disappoint Daddy? She shook her head to clear her thoughts. "This isn't about my father."

"It's always been about your father and the hopes

we had for you. The prayers we said. And it's about our Heavenly Father—''

''This isn't about anyone but *you.* All your plans have been about what *you* want. You don't care what I want.''

Laura rested a hand on her daughter's shoulder, a compassionate expression on her face. ''Sweetheart, of course I care. But you see, you can't possibly know what you want or need right now.''

''I know what I want. I want Rick.'' Charity took a deep breath, releasing an admission with her exhalation. ''I love him.'' Only as she said it did she realize with her whole heart it was true. Even the terror in confessing it couldn't compete with that rush of exhilaration.

Jerking her hand away, Laura shook her head wildly. ''No…no. You're not thinking clearly. Can't you see he's just trying to confuse you?''

''You're wrong, Mother.'' Charity held her hands wide. ''The only thing in this world I'm not confused about is that I want to be with Rick.''

Laura raised both hands as if appealing toward Heaven. ''If your father were alive, he'd know what to do with you.''

''My father?'' Although Charity tried to steady her voice, it still sounded unnatural. ''Well, he isn't alive. He died, Mother. Years ago.'' She didn't know why she added, ''And his name wasn't 'your father.' It was Joseph Sims. Can't you call him by his name?''

Fury flashed in Laura's eyes. ''How dare you speak to me that way!''

Charity wondered the same herself. How could she be so insulting to her own mother, no matter how wrong Laura was about Rick? Nothing gave her the right to say such horrible things. "Mother, I—"

Laura turned away. "You have no right to criticize me. You don't know anything about it."

Gripping her mother's shoulders from behind, she pleaded, "But I want to know. Please tell me about Daddy. Tell me he forgot your birthday. That at least once he came home late from work. Tell me he had faults and wasn't this superhuman husband that no man in my life can measure up to."

"You want me to tell you something?" Laura faced her again. "I'll tell you that either you walk away from this un-churched man, or you'll regret it forever."

"Why won't you just tell me about my father?"

"One of these days, you'll hate Mr. McKinley enough to wish him dead, too."

Accustomed to being first to arrive each morning at the construction site, Rick was surprised just after sunrise to see any vehicle in the church parking lot, let alone Charity's car. His pulse quickened at the prospect of seeing her before he processed the reality that something had to be wrong. And he had a pretty good idea it had to do with Laura.

Charity rushed up to the truck when he parked and opened the door. "Oh, Rick, you're here."

He climbed down and pressed his hands on her

shoulders. "Charity, what is it? Did something happen after I left last night?"

She shook her head. "No…not really. Yes. Oh…I don't know."

"Wait. Slow down." He needed to make some sense of her conversation and to remove the panicked expression from her face. "Tell me what happened."

"Mother and I argued."

That was a given, but he didn't want to point that out and rattle her further. "And?"

"I've been up all night. I couldn't sleep." She glanced up at him. "It was something she said."

Laura had probably said a lot of things, none of them likely flattering toward him. But Charity didn't start listing them, so he squeezed her shoulders gently until she finally looked at him. "Tell me what she said."

"It doesn't make any sense. I've got to be wrong." She backed away until she was out of his reach and shook her head hard. "I must have misunderstood."

Rick stepped forward again, but he forced himself not to touch her. "Charity, please tell me what she said."

Suddenly, her gaze seemed to clear. "I need to know if you'll help me."

"What do you mean?" he said, dropping his hands.

"I have to go to Indiana to see the death certificate. I have to know the truth."

"What truth? You're not making any sense."

"I have to go. Can you come with me or not?" She looked at him incredulously, as if he was an imbecile for failing to understand her. "I have reason to believe my mother murdered my father."

Charity walked out the doors of the Delaware County Building late that afternoon and plopped down on the steps, sighing heavily. It seemed more like days than just several hours since they'd piled into his truck and started driving south. Charity had even phoned her nursing supervisor from the road to take time off from work.

Rick longed to pull her into his arms as he lowered himself to the step just above hers, but she appeared as fragile as blown glass, and he worried she would shatter. He was surprised when he rested a hand on her shoulder that she didn't. "Are you okay?"

She straightened as if pulling on inner strength she was only beginning to recognize in herself. "They're wrong, that's all. There has to be some mistake."

There was a mistake, all right, but it probably wasn't the fault of the Delaware County Health Department. "Didn't the lady in the Vital Statistics Division say their death records date back to 1882? Even if you had the date wrong, it still should be there."

"I don't have the date wrong. They're wrong."

"Wait. What if the accident was in Madison County or Randolph or Jay?" Okay, he was grasping at straws, but he'd reach for anything if it could take the pained expression off her face. He took both of her hands and turned her to face him. "Remember, the lady said if you died someplace besides inside the county, your death certificate would be there instead of here.''

She shook her head and pulled her hands away. ''But it was here. Mother said it was here.''

They weren't talking about the location where Joseph Sims died, or even the date, and Rick knew it. They were talking about *how,* and he didn't have any answers for her. Yet in his heart of hearts, he didn't believe Charity's mother capable of murder—unless she could have accomplished it with censuring words or glares. The stuff she'd used so successfully on her daughter.

''Just because your mom hinted she might have wished your father dead doesn't mean she killed him.''

The weak smile she gave him hinted she appreciated his effort. If only he had some real experience with trusting his own parents so that he could better understand what she must have worried was a betrayal. His experience lay only in the second part, but for Charity, all of this was new.

''Thanks for saying that,'' she said as she rose from the steps. ''You've been so great today. And I really am grateful to you for coming with me. I feel bad about making you drive all morning to get here, missing work, especially when you're already behind.''

As if that pile of cement, wood, steel and brick could in any way compare to his need to protect her from all her monsters, real or imagined. If she needed answers, he wanted to find them for her. If she needed a champion, he wanted to *be* that for her. ''Remember, I insisted on driving. And if you apologize one more time, I'm going to drive away and leave you wandering around downtown Muncie.''

''Fine. Fine.''

He reached for her hand. ''This really would have been easier if you'd just looked through your mother's records.''

''You know I couldn't invade her privacy. Besides, she probably keeps it in her safety deposit box. Did you expect me to break into the bank, too?''

''It would have saved us a four-hour drive, but then going to jail doesn't sound like the best idea, either. That *really* would put us past our deadline.''

Charity couldn't help chuckling when he joined her on the sidewalk, but the truth was he had pushed his deadline even further back for her. And now here he was giving her mother the benefit of a doubt, something Mother had never given him.

''No, we wouldn't want to do that,'' she said. ''I wonder how Rusty and the rest of the guys are doing today.''

''The guys are probably wrestling a drill out of Rusty's hands as we speak,'' Rick answered with a grin.

Warmth filled her heart at she thought of the kindness Rick had shown his foreman. Like Rusty, she was lucky that Rick had taken a chance on her. Rick's presence there brought her so much comfort. Already, it seemed like a hundred years since he'd held her in his arms so tenderly, and yet it was only hours. And here he was reaching out to her again in another way.

If she hadn't already fallen in love with him, she would have been in jeopardy of tumbling head over heels right now, just from his concern. In a movement as natural for her as breathing, she turned and reached up to kiss his cheek. "Thank you."

"What was that for?" Rick said but didn't wait for her to answer before turning his mouth and brushing hers. "Okay, now what? You're sure you have the place right?"

"How many times do you think Mother told me that story?" When he glanced over at her, Charity smiled. "Believe me, I'm right."

"Then I don't know what to do next."

She let Rick help her into the passenger seat, having no better ideas than he did. When inspiration struck, she hopped out of the car and bumped heads with him. "I think I've got it."

Rick rubbed his temple. "What—besides a headache?"

But she ignored his joke and her throbbing forehead, the wheels of an idea turning in her mind. "Okay, let's just say that the Delaware County Health Department made a mistake just this once, and Daddy's death certificate was misfiled. There's another place where we can find information about an auto accident."

"Where's that?"

"The library. They'll have copies of old newspapers on microfilm. If there was an accident that day, a fatality, in this area, it would be in the paper."

Anticipation filled her at the thought of putting this mystery to rest, but misgivings nibbled at the edges of her confidence. What would it mean if they came up empty at the library?

Chapter Fourteen

"It isn't in there...anywhere," Charity said as she scanned the old, microfilmed copy of the *Star* for the third time. Over her shoulder she saw Rick shrug, his expression perplexed. Finally, she shut off the machine.

Rick didn't look at her as he removed the film from the collection spools and returned it to its metal case. If only he would look her way. She needed something stable in this horrible sea of variables, and the honesty in his eyes was the only certainty she could imagine. His faith in her was the only thing she could trust.

"Okay, what do we know for sure?" she said mostly to herself. "My father didn't die that day in Delaware County or any surrounding county that might have been in the newspaper's coverage area. Or die *any* day in that particular county. That's all we know, right?" She wished she understood only that, nothing more. She hated the list of possible scenarios lining up in her consciousness like a firing squad with guns, all trained on her.

"I don't know, Charity. Are you ready to give up?"

She shook her head. Not yet. Not when answers might be waiting if she only stretched her hand one more inch to reach for them. "Wait. I have one more idea. I know it's a long shot, but new technology might save us after all. Let's check the Internet."

When they'd settled at one of the library's computer terminals a few minutes later, Charity had already convinced herself that a computer search was as futile as the rest of their so-called research. How she'd mistaken the dates and places from her mother's stories she couldn't imagine, but obviously she had.

"Well, here goes." She typed the name Joseph Ronald Sims into the people search division of the search engine, purposely looking at Rick while the computer worked. Her stomach clenched the same way it had while they'd searched for death certificates and while they'd scanned rolls of microfilm. "It won't show anything."

"You know, there's probably more than one Joseph R. Sims in the world, anyway."

His comment would have seemed no more than sympathetic were Rick not staring at the screen. Charity turned back to the monitor. Sure enough, the world had more than its share of men named Joseph Sims. Several even had the same initial. But only one had the exact name, including middle name Ronald, and he just happened to live in a city not thirty minutes from Muncie.

"Anderson, Indiana?" Rick read over her shoulder. "Isn't that really close to here?"

She nodded, pressing back the panic that squeezed her throat. His fingers felt cool as he brushed them along the side of her cheek until she turned back to him.

"It could be a coincidence. This doesn't mean it's him," Rick told her, voicing her rationalizations and her fears when she wasn't ready to do it.

Charity stared at the address until its numbers and letters blurred. The name could have meant nothing— words connected by no more than the thinnest branches of genealogical trees and lack of creativity by parents naming their children. Still, she couldn't ignore the suspicion that infested her thoughts and then blanketed them.

"It doesn't seem possible. Or could it be?" She asked herself and Rick at the same time. Then her thoughts settled clearly. "If there's a chance my father could be alive, I want to know the truth."

Futile hope and anger vied for supremacy in her thoughts a short while later as Charity pushed the doorbell to the modest home in Anderson, Indiana. She waited for someone, who could quite possibly be the world's biggest liar, to answer the door. If this man was her father, and that still was a huge *if,* how could he have been so cruel as to let her believe he was dead? That ridiculous childhood dream—the one where Daddy's death had been only a horrible mistake—reared its ugly head, crippling her determination to know the truth, whatever it was.

She glanced back at Rick, who stood on the step just below her, and he squeezed her shoulder. His support behind her gave her the strength to stay put when her survival instinct told her to run.

For several seconds no one answered, so Charity pressed the bell again. A graying man pulled open the door. "Hello. May I help—" He stopped midsentence and stared, his jaw slack.

Vague familiarity crawled over her at the sight of his hazel eyes and straight nose, and bile rose to the back of her throat. Did he really look like the shrine of pictures arranged in her mother's house, or was her mind just playing tricks on her?

The pause dragged on, the man beyond the half-opened door appearing stricken, his gaze focused on her. She could have sworn he took in each of her features separately and then studied how they combined to form her face. When she could bear his scrutiny no longer without screaming, she asked in a voice even she didn't recognize, "Are you Joseph Ronald Sims?"

The man coughed against his fist, his skin pallid. "Yes, I am. Who are you?" He stepped outside the storm door and allowed it to fall closed behind him.

The voice. This time when she heard him speak, memories of laughter, of lullabies, assaulted her. Were they real or imagined? Was it even this voice she'd heard? This time she fought the temptation to mourn the loss of moments so few that she'd hoarded them like treasured heirlooms. "My questions first." She kept her voice steady, but her hands shook, so she stuffed them in her jeans pockets. "Are you or are you not the father of a Charity Lynne Sims?"

"I—"

"And if you are this person, why would you allow your child to believe you were dead all these years?" She couldn't even look at him anymore, not when his face metamorphosed under her stare into that young, smiling image in those pictures emblazoned on her memory. Would he lie now that she already knew the truth?

"Yes, Charity, I'm *your* father."

He'd recognized her though she hadn't said her name. And like her, he knew. At once, white dots as from a flash camera danced before her eyes. Her head swam. Because anger seemed the closest thing to reality in this surreal scene, Charity clasped it with both hands.

"How dare you disappear and let me believe—" She stopped as her screeching voice echoed across the line of small, but well-tended houses.

"Please, let me explain," the man said in a strained voice as he lifted a hand to touch her.

Charity backed away before he could graze her cheek. Jerking her head one way and the other, she searched for anything steady in a world that had crumbled through an invisible fault line.

Then she saw him.

The man she loved stepped from behind her to her

side, putting his arm around her and squeezing her shoulder. Rick held her in one still, safe place, while everything else around them moved in and out of focus.

"Let's go inside, and then you can start... explaining, that is." Rick indicated with his head toward the door.

"I'm Joe Sims."

Rick forced himself to accept the man's proffered hand, though he wanted more than anything to reject the man on Charity's behalf. *And I'm the man who loves her,* Rick wanted to yell. But he only said, "Rick McKinley," as he opened the door. Charity just stood there, her face pale, her eyes filled with an eerie, glassy look. As if she'd seen a ghost.

In effect, she had.

Rick took her hand, trying not to notice how lifeless her fingers remained as he pulled her inside. So docile, so unlike the Charity who had captured his heart, she let him lead her to the sofa. Rick wanted to strike out at the man and the situation that made her feel so helpless.

"Let's say you're Charity's biological father. Then where have you been the last twenty-seven years?" His jaw ached from gritting his teeth.

"Well, I..." The man let his words drift away, dropping into the recliner across from the sofa and curling his shoulders forward. His eyes, a green-brown combination similar to Charity's, appeared wet. "Where do I begin?"

Rick didn't care where he started as long as the

man said something that could draw Charity out of her disconnected state. He took her hand, squeezed it, but still felt no response.

"First, do you have proof that you two are related?" Not that he really needed it, especially given the way Charity had reacted to him. But he hoped seeing something tangible would bring her out of her daze.

"I have a copy of her birth certificate," Joseph said.

Instead of standing to retrieve the document from some lock box or filing cabinet, Joseph simply reached for his wallet. From inside it, he produced a yellowed paper and tossed it on the coffee table. As crinkled as it appeared, he must have carried it around for years.

Charity lowered her gaze to the certificate, but she didn't become instantly alert, as Rick had hoped. Tempted to shake her awake and cradle her in his arms, he resisted by studying the document and then fingering its parchment.

"You carry this in your wallet, you live not a half hour away from your old home, and yet you never came after your own child?"

An anguished sound rushed from Joseph's lungs, and he shoved both hands through his hair, leaving gray-brown locks in disarray. He didn't even try push them back down.

"Don't you think it's about time she heard the truth?" Rick closed his fingers over Charity's hand again, not convinced she was ready to hear what her father had to say.

Joseph closed his eyes for several seconds before he lifted his head and pushed his shoulders back. "Yes, it's time. Laura and I had marital problems right from the beginning, but when we divorced, I moved from Muncie to Anderson. Close enough to still see my daughter, but away from her mother."

"Divorced?" Rick stressed the word, hoping to get a response from Charity, but she just sat there.

Joseph breathed deeply and continued. "Then one day when I went to pick up my daughter, the house was empty."

"They'd just disappeared?" Rick prompted, watching Charity through his peripheral vision. Still no reaction.

"I didn't know where Laura had taken her. That's when she must have moved to Milford, Michigan."

Charity jerked her hand from Rick's grasp. "You knew?" she shrieked. "All this time, you knew where I was, and you never came for me?"

"Sweetheart, it was years before I found you again," Joseph said, his hands held wide, "and by then I didn't know what lies your mother had told—"

"No!" Rick and Charity both shouted at the same time, but only she only kept shaking her head so hard that tresses slipped from her ponytail.

Rick's need to defend her brought him to his feet, his hands fisted. Because his lines of right and wrong blurred just when they needed to crystallize, he held those errant hands to his sides. "You're not going to get off that easily, blaming Mrs. Sims.'' *No matter how culpable she was,* his mind added without permission. ''Charity has believed all her life that her father was dead, and it's your fault she doesn't know differently.''

Joseph pressed his forefinger and thumb to the bridge of his nose, and when he lowered his hand, tears spilled over his lower lids.

''I know it's my fault. Only mine.'' He paused for a long time, and when he spoke again, Joseph faced his daughter, who watched him with a wary gaze.

''Charity, I'm so sorry. I never should have left you, no matter how justifiable the reasons sounded at the time.'' He wrung his hands so hard that his fingertips appeared red while other parts of his fingers flashed white. ''The letters, the calls—it doesn't matter. I should have tried harder, but after a while it became easier not to try. I kept waiting for the right time to tell you—''

She jumped to her feet. ''I'm almost thirty years old. You couldn't find *the right time* in twenty-seven years?''

''I was such a coward. Donna begged me to tell you.'' Joseph stared at the mantel, seeming to speak to himself more than to either of them. ''For the both of you.''

For the first time, Rick noticed the display of tiny silver-framed photographs across the dark slab of wood. Of a smiling brunette holding an infant, of a dark-haired little girl in a ballet costume, of a young woman in a graduation cap and gown. Charity noticed them, too, and crossed to the fireplace, picking up one after another.

She turned back to them. "Who are these people?"

"My late wife, Donna, and our daughter, Julia." Joseph licked his lips before continuing. "Your sister."

Rick shot another glance at the row of pictures. This Julia was as dark as Charity was fair, but their features were amazingly similar.

"A sister?" She stared at the pictures again, her mouth agape.

Joseph walked up behind her and lifted his hand close to her shoulder but then lowered it, as if he realized how unwelcome his touch would be. "Two years after the divorce, I married Donna. It took us five years, but we finally had a baby girl." He glanced back at the row of pictures. "She's twenty-one, and she'll graduate from the University of Iowa in the spring."

"And your wife?" she said in a whisper.

"She passed away two years ago. Complications from diabetes."

"She knew about me?"

"Always. After we located you in Michigan, she kept a scrapbook on you with any bits of information we could find. She always encouraged me to make contact with you when you became an adult."

"I've been an adult for more than a decade."

Emotion obviously welling again, Joseph coughed into his hand. When he spoke again, he wiped away twin tears with the backs of his hands. "I'm so sorry.

Leaving you was the biggest mistake of my life. I was so ashamed I'd allowed you to be taken away that I didn't want to be a failure in Julia's eyes as well. I hoped someday she'd understand—you'd both understand—and forgive me.''

''Does she know?''

''Not yet, but I will tell her. Today.'' He glanced back and forth between the pictures and Charity— between his two children. ''You may not be able to ever forgive me, as much I pray for it. But remember, Julia has done nothing. I hope someday you'll be willing to meet her.''

''Will she want to meet me? After she finds out your little secret?''

''I know she will,'' Joseph said. ''Since her mother and I were only children, and our parents are gone now, I'm the only relative she has. Now she'll have you, too.''

Charity nodded, but she still seemed so unsure, so vulnerable. She'd had enough surprises today, without adding a sister she'd never known to the mix. The foundation of her life had been shaken, and Rick longed to make someone pay for putting her in this fragile position. For yanking the rug of confidence from beneath her feet.

''You don't have to decide about meeting her now, Charity,'' Rick said. ''Not until after you've figured out what to do about…the other.''

Charity startled as if he'd just awakened her with his words. ''You know, he's right.'' Crossing the room, she stopped in front of her father, still a careful distance out of his reach. "Where do you keep your suitcase?"

"What do you mean?" Joseph said, although his stricken expression showed he'd gotten her gist.

His daughter only pressed her lips together. "I think it's about time you faced my mother."

Chapter Fifteen

Just after midnight Charity stared at the outline of her darkened house as Rick parked the truck. After nearly five hours on the road, Charity would have thought she was ready to face her mother and the rest of this nightmare. But she wasn't ready, and wondered if she ever would be.

No number of golden wheat fields or plowed cornfields they had passed on the drive northeast through Indiana to Michigan would have been large enough to help her clear her thoughts. Not when she'd been unable to think clearly since she'd first laid eyes on Joseph Sims. Even now, every attempt to inhale only brought with it a whiff of her father's strangely familiar, musky aftershave from the truck's cramped back seat. Again, her stomach rolled.

Father.

The word made her palms damp and her insides tremble. She'd always called him Daddy, but now the word soured upon her lips. Look at the difference a few hours could make. Orphan to daughter. Only child to sister. Capable woman to confused little girl.

The steel, glass and upholstery of the truck's cab closed in around them, sandwiching her with the man she loved and the man who should have loved her as a birthright. Both seemed to want something from her. Something she couldn't give. She would suffocate soon if she didn't run, didn't escape them both.

Just when she needed space more than any sustenance, she was about to add to the crowd that contained her. As if on cue, the tiny hairs at her nape stood on end. Goose bumps decorated her arms. *Mother.* Could she survive facing the woman who had lied to her all her life?

"This is it?" Joseph said of the house, lit only by a front porch light. Instead of waiting for an answer, he continued. "The Wooley money sure paid off on this place."

"Wooley money?" By the time the question had passed her lips, she didn't need an answer. Of course, her father hadn't provided for their family since he hadn't died. That comfortable nest egg her mother had spoken of so often had come from Laura's late parents all along.

"How did you think a young widow had afforded it?"

She opened her mouth but only closed it again. The house, too, was part of the lie.

Rick pushed open his door. "Are we going in?"

"I just want to get it over with." Joseph's tone was filled with dread.

Charity could relate to that, but like him, she recognized the inevitability of this meeting. "Okay, let's go." She escaped the truck's cramped quarters and headed to a trap of another sort.

Soon, Charity stood in the doorway to her mother's bedroom, reluctant to push her way inside. "Mother, are you awake?"

"I am now." Laura sat up in bed, glancing at the clock on the bedside table. "Aren't you supposed to be at work? Is something wrong? Are you all right?"

Obviously, her mother had forgotten she wasn't speaking to her—not since she'd professed love for the "wrong" man. Laura had forgotten a few other small details as well. Like that Charity's father was very much alive.

"I'm fine, but we need to talk. Can you come downstairs right away?"

Harrumphing as she climbed out of bed and slipped into her robe, Laura followed her daughter down the stairs. Charity steadied her hand on the rail as the two men in the living room came into view, Joseph in the center and Rick in the corner rocker.

Laura's gasp punctuated the silence. She must have missed a step for she stumbled on the stairs, only catching herself by clamping onto her daughter's shoulder. "Oh, my…"

"Hello again, Laura," Joseph called out.

Charity shivered with revulsion and stepped down again to escape her mother's touch.

Joseph raised his chin, his jaw tight, before he spoke. "I don't remember you looking so pale. Are you surprised to see me...back from the dead?"

With a rustle of robes, Laura stepped around her daughter to face the ghost of her past. No residual effects of her momentary weakness showed as she straightened her shoulders and met Joseph's gaze. Only the way she fiddled with the robe belt gave her away until she dropped her hands and snorted with derision. "From the dead? You'll never return from the dead."

He took a step toward her, his hands fisted. "Well, I stand before you—and our daughter—very much alive."

Instead of backing down, Laura tilted her chin up as she reached the landing. Charity couldn't take it anymore. Didn't they see that there were consequences to their decisions? There were victims?

"Would you two stop this?" She descended the last few steps and faced Laura. "Mother, why did you lie to me? I have the right to know."

"Lied?" Laura blanched, wide-eyed, as if she didn't know the definition of the word, let alone connect it to sin. "It wasn't really a lie. Your father was *dead to me* from the moment he left us, serving me with those despicable divorce papers."

Charity's thoughts whirled, but she focused on the anger to find control. "Not a lie? Not a lie?" She heard her pitch grow higher, but she couldn't stop it. Then another thought eclipsed the building diatribe.

"Wait. 'Your father.' Rick was the one who pointed out it was what you always called him."

She paused to look at the man they both spoke of. "Never Joseph. Never Joe, or even Daddy. You never referred to him by name, and I only thought that meant his death still hurt too much after all those years."

Laura shook her head so hard her whole upper body moved before looking directly at Joseph. "He didn't deserve a name."

"Why?" Joseph asked through gritted teeth. "Because I couldn't take it anymore after you stood in front of the church congregation and lied? You told them I was becoming a preacher—just like you'd always wanted." His arms and his hands clenched and unclenched at his sides. "I was already serving as a deacon *for you,* when I wasn't even ready to commit my life to God. It just wasn't enough, was it?"

Laura shrugged. "You always were a disappointment."

But Joseph ignored her comment and kept talking. "I was so humiliated. I couldn't live a lie anymore. Not in front of my daughter or God."

"You left," Laura snarled. "You deserted your wife and child without a second thought."

"Sounds to me, Mrs. Sims, like his leaving was more gift to you than tragedy."

Charity startled at the sound of Rick's voice behind her. How could she have forgotten his presence when his support had only been a few steps away? Still, for some reason, she couldn't reach out to him, even as he stepped to her and rested a hand on her shoulder.

"You don't know—" Laura began, but Rick stopped her with a wave of his hand.

"His absence allowed you to play the role of poor widow and to give your daughter this imaginary saint of a father she would fear disappointing. That kept Charity under your control—just where you wanted her."

Rick squeezed Charity's shoulder in a symbol of comfort, but she couldn't accept its relief. Nothing could help her now. She jerked her arm, and with a sidelong glance, he dropped his hand away but stayed close by. Why couldn't she appreciate his constancy when the rest of her world had become fluid?

Slowly, Charity turned back to the woman who'd constructed the house of lies they both had lived in for far too long. "The rest of the story, Mother. Are you saying none of it was a lie? Do you even know how to tell the truth?"

"Yes, Laura, tell her the truth about how you moved to Michigan so I wouldn't find you," Joseph said, folding his arms across his chest. "Tell her how when I did find you, you refused to take my calls, even getting an unlisted number. And tell her why I have a crate of returned letters at home."

Rather than face Joseph and his accusations, Laura turned to her daughter alone. "I did it all for you, sweetheart. Can't you see that? I had to protect you."

"From me?"

"From Daddy?" Charity shot a glance at him after their comments trampled each other. She swallowed hard and saw his Adam's apple jerk. The word *daddy,* spoken aloud and dangling in the air, had shocked them both.

"No, no, no." Laura shook her head, tears forging trails down her cheeks. "I didn't want you to make the same mistake I did…falling for the wrong type of man." She paused, sniffling, but still managed to toss Rick a venomous look. "But you did it, anyway."

Charity tightened her shoulders and glanced at Rick. If the admission buried in Laura's insult had thrown him off balance, he gave no indication. Instead, he stepped closer to Charity, wrapping an arm around her shoulders. His unspoken message was clear: He wasn't going anywhere. Yet that surety only made her feel more claustrophobic.

"I was the wrong type?" Joseph said, his jaw tightening. "What about you—"

"No, you…"

Her parents continued spouting ugly accusations, but it all became white noise as she tuned out the pain. They weren't debating trivial matters. This was her life they were talking about. A life that used to make sense.

Would anything ever be clear again? Hopelessness seeped through her mind and flooded the crevices of her soul. The sensation of sinking pulled her arms and legs, tempting her to fall into a heap in the floor. She had to fight it. Had to step away from the lies, the expectations that crowded this house to the walls.

Run!

Until the word ripped through her thoughts, she hadn't formulated a plan, and she certainly didn't pause to do it. Shaking her shoulder until Rick's arm fell away, she rushed toward the door. *But you left your car at the church.*

Panic threatened until she spied Rick's jacket hanging on the corner coat tree alongside her purse. She dived for them, grabbing the truck keys and pushing through the front door. She didn't look back until she was inside the truck and only its taillights illuminated the house that was no longer a home.

"Charity! Stop! Please!" Rick hollered as he hurried down the steps. But she'd already pulled into the street and had gunned the engine.

His heart squeezing in his chest, he raced down the driveway, anyway, as if his cross-trainers could compete with steel-belted radials and a V-8 engine. By the time he reached the street, she'd driven over the hill and out of sight. He turned and sprinted back to the house.

Lord, please let her be okay.

He stormed back inside. "She's gone. Are either of you going to do anything?"

Joseph stood at the picture window, the curtain yanked back. Laura stared out at the blackness from the same spot where she'd stood when Charity had run out. No more than a few minutes had passed, yet it felt like an eternity.

"Are you just going to stand there?" He stalked over to Joseph. "She's getting farther away."

"We shouldn't have let her get out the door," Laura said, leaving little doubt that Rick was the culpable "we" she spoke of. "She's in no shape to drive."

"But you're going to do nothing about it now?" Joseph answered. "You've lied to her all her life and yet—"

"Stop it! Stop it!" Rick raised both hands into the air emphatically. "Would you two stop fighting? Could you forget about yourselves and think about your daughter?"

Startled, Laura and Joseph turned back to him.

Joseph squeezed his eyes shut and nodded when he reopened them. "He's right. We've got to go after her."

"I'll need your car, Mrs. Sims," Rick said, pacing away from them and back. "Charity has my truck."

"I'm coming with you," Joseph said, grabbing his coat.

When Laura strode into the kitchen, Rick fought to keep himself from chasing after her and wrestling the keys from her. But to his surprise, she hurried back, a key chain dangling from her fingers. She tossed it to him.

"You two go," Laura said. "I'll stay here in case she comes to her senses and returns. You'll keep me updated from your cell phone?"

Rick nodded over his shoulder and headed toward the garage. Joseph followed him out the door.

"Do you know where she might have gone?" Joseph said as he climbed in the passenger door of the silver Lincoln.

The car already in reverse, Rick backed down the curved drive to the street. "I have a few ideas."

Several turns through the hilly subdivision led them to Milford Road. Rick looked north then south, determining the best direction to go. He had to figure out where she had gone to hide from the lies her mother had told—and her father had taken far too long to refute. *Lord, please let me find her. I'll never let them hurt her again.*

"I'm sure she'll be okay, Rick."

Until Joseph spoke, Rick hadn't noticed how quiet it had become inside the car. "You're probably right."

"Of course I am." The nervous way Charity's father shifted in his seat suggested he wasn't convinced. "My daughter has a good head on her shoulders."

The hairs on the back of Rick's neck stood as he watched his passenger with his peripheral vision, but he fought for a clear head. Still he couldn't resist asking, "Who told you that? You can't be certain of anything about your daughter. She's a stranger to you."

Joseph cleared his throat and fiddled with the buttons on the armrest until the window opened. "You're right about that. And I'm a stranger to her—at least for now. But I do know one thing about her. She was smart enough to fall in love with you."

Rick's foot hit the brakes of its own volition, the tires screeching. He checked his rearview mirror, grateful no one had been tailgating. Why did everyone keep assuming something Charity had never admitted herself? Come to think of it, he'd never said it to her, either, no matter how true it was.

"You love her, too."

Joseph had spoken the words as fact, not even bothering to ask, so Rick couldn't understand why he felt compelled to answer. "Charity's this amazing person. So smart. So funny. So impassioned, even in her misguided approach to…God." Choking over his inability to stop singing her praises, he shrugged and stared at the lines on the dark pavement ahead.

Her father said nothing, seeming content to let the subject die a slow death, falling to rest on the smooth, leather upholstery.

Only it wouldn't die. When the silence in the car's interior grew loud enough to overcome noises outside, Rick gripped the steering wheel and glanced at the other man. "Yes, I love her."

Charity lifted her head from the truck's steering wheel and ground fists into her burning, swollen eyes as two headlights approached in the church drive. As the lights drew nearer, she recognized her mother's car.

"Oh, Mother," she exhaled but straightened and brushed furiously at her cheeks, as if doing so could remove evidence from a three-hour crying jag.

Since Charity expected Laura's backlit form to emerge from the car door, the driver's masculine shoulders surprised her. Long before she could make out his face, she recognized Rick's carriage and stature. He tore over to the truck, bracing his hands on the window she'd left open though she was freezing.

"Thank God, you're all right. I was so worried. We looked everywhere…twice. It's after four o'clock."

His words confused her as they came in a rush.

But one thing stuck in her mind. "Did you say *we?*" Clearing her throat, she focused on the car that he'd left running. It looked empty.

"You're father and I drove around for hours. I finally convinced him to let me take him to a hotel, but he made me promise I'd call as soon as I found you."

"My father?" she asked, finally meeting his gaze. Even after so many hours, it still sounded strange to mouth those words that so many children took for granted. How unfair it was that she still couldn't accept with joy the parent she'd long been denied.

He nodded and turned his head toward the parsonage. "If not for Andrew…"

"I should have known he'd report on me when I noticed him nosing around. If only I'd remembered. He always tinkers with that old Harley in his barn at night." If she'd been thinking straight, she would have wondered why Andrew had paused nearby but hadn't approached the truck to check on her. But she'd been nowhere close to thinking straight. Otherwise, she would have climbed into her own car and started driving again. It was still parked where she'd left it the morning before. "He called you?"

"No, he called your mother back. She stayed at the

house in case you returned, but she must have phoned several church members, searching for you.''

Charity swallowed hard, tears threatening again, no matter how determined she was not to let him see them. She resisted the urge to pity her mother. No, she wasn't ready to feel anything. Yet she felt everything and nothing, combined in a mass that threatened to strangle her with its sheer volume of tentacles.

''So you've found me.''

''Where did you go?''

Away from all of you. But she only said, ''I just kept driving around on the back roads. Then I came here.''

''I'm glad you came back.''

Tempted to seek comfort in his words, she remembered that nothing could heal her broken life. ''What now?''

''I want my truck back, and I want to get you back home, though not necessarily in that order.''

''Oh...sorry,'' she said, glancing about the truck cab that no longer seemed the safe haven it had been for the last few hours while she'd driven without a destination.

''Do you want me to get Andrew to drive your mom's car, so I can drive the truck? We'll pick up yours later.''

''No, I can manage.''

He turned to study her. ''Are you sure you can drive?''

''I'm sure.'' The lie tasted bitter on her tongue. She

would never feel sure about anything again. "I'm... fine." But her voice broke, giving her away.

Although Rick had seen through all of her bravado, the collapse of her pretense still rocked him as if the sobs sprang from his own heart. And that ache wouldn't stop until he could gather her in his arms. He jerked the door open and bent to hold her before he could worry about whether she would push away his compassion.

"Charity, honey, you're not okay," he crooned into her hair. "They were wrong. You're parents were so wrong in the things they did and said."

"I just don't understand."

"How could you? I don't know how anyone could be so selfish as to walk away from his child without fighting for her or to let her daughter mourn the way she did."

Her only answer was a heartbreaking sob. Rick scooted her across the seat so he could sit next to her, absorbing the force of her misery, his jacket damp with tears.

He hadn't been there to comfort her in the imaginary loss of her father, but now he rocked her in the tragedy of finding him. She'd paid dearly for the *gift* of having Joseph return to her life with everything she'd ever believed true.

"Honey, I'm sorry they lied to you."

Pushing back, Charity pressed her fingertips to the bridge of her nose and stared into the darkness, interrupted only by the Lincoln's headlights. "I don't know what to believe anymore. My whole life is a lie.''

Rick gripped her shoulders until she looked at him. ''That's not true. So many things in your life are true. You're a wonderful nurse. Your patients love you.''

She kept shaking her head, her quiet tears glistening in the light flooding the cab, but he couldn't stop. He had to make her see what he saw in her. What had been there all along, no matter how hard she'd tried to hide it. ''You're good and kind. Smart and funny. You're caring and worthy of being loved.''

''No, I'm worthy of nothing. I just can't believe—''

''Then believe this. I love you. Just you. The way you are.'' He rested his fingertips beneath her chin and leaned in to seal the promise of his heart with a kiss. But she jerked her head back from either shock or aversion. He tried not to feel the sting of her rejection.

''Why? Why would you love me?''

Shoving his hands back through his hair, Rick leaned his head against the back of the seat. ''Oh, Charity. How could I not? You challenge me to be more than I am. You make me believe that God answers prayer.''

The space she put between them by moving to the passenger door seemed more like a ravine compared to the canyon she created in emotional distance. The need to pull her back, to beg her not to leave him, pressed him so hard that he gripped the steering wheel to stop himself.

"You can't love me," she said, staring out the window. "You don't even know me. Not the real me. Nobody does."

"I know you. I see through this wall you have built to protect yourself. I saw it that first day I met you."

"Whatever you think you know, you're wrong. This *real me* you speak of doesn't exist. Just like the orphan Charity never existed."

Rick released the wheel, reaching for a hand that she jerked from him. "Please don't pull away. You need someone right now. Let me be that person."

"I can't." Her hand already rested on the door. "I just can't. Needing is too hard…scary…too much."

By the time he heard her say, "Sorry," she'd already pushed the door open and had stepped to the ground.

"Charity, don't go," he called after her as he climbed down to follow. *Don't leave me,* the deserted little boy inside him cried out in silence.

Chapter Sixteen

Rick's footsteps shuffled behind her, yet Charity couldn't force herself to slow. She had to get away. *What are you running from?* The question hammered inside her brain, its answer as elusive as her former life.

But a dead end formed before her as she reached for the door handle of her own car. Her purse was still in the truck. She glanced at the car that Rick had left running. If she took it, she would have to face her mother and return it. Obviously that was inevitable, but she wanted to delay that as long as she could.

Frantic, she pulled open her unlocked door, flooding the car with light. If only she'd left her keys in the ignition. Now there was no easy escape from Rick or from the jumble of confusing feelings that squeezed her heart.

With both fists, she pounded on the car's roof and

lowered her head to the cool metal of the door frame. He approached behind her, his nearness a contradiction in its comfort and its disquiet.

"You'll need this to make your getaway." He held her purse out to her. "That is, if you want to keep running."

His statement tried and convicted her in a single breath, but she couldn't allow herself to be trapped by it. Not when the car keys and the space she needed more than oxygen were within her reach. "Thanks." She turned just enough to clasp the purse, but he raised it above his head.

"Just give it to me...please."

They both stared up at the suspended handbag for a few seconds until he finally lowered it into her grasp.

"Could I have the truck keys back?"

Digging into her jacket pocket, she withdrew them, but as she attempted to drop them into his hand without a brush of skin, he lifted his arm. Even the cool metal mashed between their palms failed to stop the warmth that spread through her as he curled his fingers over the back of her hand. That warmth threatened to touch her soul.

But she couldn't let it.

"Charity, I know your life is crazy now. But that doesn't mean you have to walk away from me." He closed his other hand over her forearm, squeezing it with a reassurance that only caused new tears to cloud her vision.

"I just don't know—"

"I think we have a chance for something real. Something permanent." He paused until she finally met his gaze. "I want that. Don't you?"

Only with every beat of my heart. Despair washed over her, and the plea in his eyes tore through her heart. He needed her. But she couldn't afford to be needed right now. She had nothing to give. "Don't you see? I can't. How can I build any kind of relationship with you when I don't know who I am?"

"You don't have to prove anything to me."

"How could I when I don't know anything about myself?"

Rick gripped her shoulders, his face only inches from hers. "When your mother suggested that you loved me, you didn't deny it."

The rush of tears came so quickly she had no time to fight them. She jerked her head back and swiped her face with her jacket sleeve. When she answered, she stared at the gravel beneath her feet. "No...I didn't."

"Shouldn't that make a difference?"

All she could do was shake her head. "It doesn't. It can't. I can't be with you, Rick. Not with anyone."

She backed into the seat and away from him and the hope he dangled before her in her hopeless world. But before she could close the door, he stepped once more into the arc of its opening. Crouching low, he rested a hand on her arm, his touch more comforting than she deserved.

"You're not going to let me help you. Maybe I

couldn't help anyway.'' He released a long sigh. ''But I know somebody who can.''

She pushed away the temptation to believe these wrongs could be made right. ''No one can help.''

''God can if you'll trust Him. He never lied to you, and He never will.''

Again, she shook her head, so hard this time that her neck ached. ''You don't understand.''

''But He does. God is waiting for you when you're ready. He wants you to open your heart to Him.''

Standing and stepping away, he pushed her door shut. Without looking back, he crossed to her mother's car and parked it before climbing into his pickup. If he glanced at her before driving away, she missed it.

''Goodbye, Rick.'' But as she watched the tail-lights disappear through the veil of her tears and into the blackness of remaining night, she'd never felt so lost. So completely alone.

The day's first sunlight streamed into her hotel room window by the time Charity bolted the door and closed the blinds. It seemed so strange to be there in this artificial bedroom not twenty minutes away from where her regular bed waited, but she couldn't go back. Laura's house was no longer her home.

The thought that she'd have to face her mother eventually to pick up her clothes only added to her exhaustion. She made her way to one of the dark-spread-covered double beds and collapsed.

How strange that no tears came, though her eyes

still burned. Crying was useless, anyway, incapable of righting wrongs or rolling back the clock to periods of blissful ignorance. Or bringing back forsaken loves.

Nothing can help you now. The thought made the room seem enormous, emphasized her isolation. Closing her eyes, she buried her face in an overstuffed pillow and settled into her doom. If she could only stop hearing what Rick had said. "But I know somebody who can." Could God really make this impossible situation right?

And that part about when she was ready to open her heart—what had he meant by that? What did Rick know? Even though he was well-versed in Scripture, she could still probably teach him a thing or two about the Word. But even as she thought it, she knew it was a lie. Maybe she could recite the names of the King James Version's sixty-six books in order and quote the verses on the "Roman Road to Salvation," but she sensed Rick had more faith in his pinky finger than she possessed in her whole heart.

She was so jealous of that pinky.

Rolling over, she sat up in bed and glanced at the television, but the Bible on the nightstand drew her attention instead. Maybe the Scriptures would comfort her this time, the way they used to, instead of compounding her emptiness as they had lately.

With the book in her lap, she flipped through several New Testament passages she knew by heart— "for God so loved the world," and "for by grace are you saved," and "but the gift of God is eternal life."

The words should have comforted her in their familiarity, but they shocked her instead. It was as if she
was reading them for the first time. As if they had
been written just for her. A verse in the tiny book of
Titus spoke the loudest.

"'Not by works of righteousness which we have
done,'" she read in a whisper, "'but according to his
mercy…'"

His mercy? That meant none of it—Sunday school
teaching, Wednesday prayer services, the Thursday
night visitation—had made any difference. New
tears—this time filled with regret—stung her eyes.
Her cheeks felt raw as the hot tears skimmed her
skin's surface. How could she have missed the message before?

She'd been too busy comparing herself to the rest
of the congregation, measuring their good deeds
against hers, their infractions against her personal
measuring stick. And she'd been too busy accusing
Andrew and Serena of sin to ever study her own heart.

Until now.

And at this moment, her heart ached with emptiness. No longer could she bear the void inside her.
She'd believed the message of Jesus' death and res-
urrection in her head, but all this time she'd been
trying to earn the salvation God promised. With all
her efforts, she'd only been spitting into the wind.
Only God's mercy mattered.

*Father, why didn't I see it before? Why did I try
so hard?* She closed the hardcover Bible, staring

down at its gold-embossed letters. *Rick said You've been waiting for me. Is he right?*

Thank you for him, by the way. She gasped as her heart squeezed with the mixed emotions of love and loss. *He has been such a gift.* A sob escaped from deep inside her chest, pain following its escape through her throat. Could she survive? She must. And suddenly she realized with God's help she would.

"Father, I know I've made You wait an awfully long time," she whispered. "Thank You for not giving up on me. I'm here now. Just me. I want to know You the way Rick knows You. I need to feel You in my heart."

At once, a calm rushed through her, so different from any she'd known. "Thank you, God." The words rushed from her lungs.

Was this what peace felt like? So warm, so filled with hope, when all evidence pointed to the contrary? Was this true faith? Believing in what she couldn't see? Knowing for certain it was real? She lowered her head to the pillow and closed her eyes, feeling for the first time that all things were possible.

"Hey, boss, you finally showed," Chuck called out early that afternoon as Rick climbed down from his pickup. The crew member paused long enough to bite into his sandwich before continuing over a mouthful, "We figured you and that feisty blonde had eloped or something."

The violent look Rick tossed at his employee must have hit its mark because Chuck hopped off the tailgate where he'd been eating and excused himself to the portable outhouse. The guy deserved as much for hitting below the belt.

"Come on, guys. Get back to work," Rusty called out from the other side of the structure.

"Let's get on it," Rick agreed. "We need to finish sheathing the walls today, or we'll have subcontractors twiddling their thumbs next week."

"Shouldn't you get some rest?" Rusty asked as he approached.

"I slept a few hours." He hadn't wanted to come at all and he still wanted to jump back in his truck and leave this place in a trail of exhaust. This project only served as a reminder of everything he'd lost. And how unlikely he was to ever experience love like that again. He wouldn't be able to look at the new building without seeing Charity there, planting her flowers. Or the way she'd looked early that morning. Betrayed. Confused. Yet certain she couldn't accept any help—or love—from him.

"You okay, boss?" another crew member who didn't value his life much called out.

Rick glanced down. He had to look stupid standing in the center of the floor, his hammer dangling from his hand. With a quick jerk of his arm, he tucked the tool back through the hammer loop attached to his jeans. Tucking thoughts of Charity away would be a hundred times harder, but he planned to do that, too.

You were a loner, remember? It was about time he figured out how to act like one again, even if it killed him. Not a far stretch when his heart already had died.

"Rick, are the doors ready to be hung?" Chuck called out, obviously over his fit of cowardice.

"They will be…after we stop talking and start sheathing." He yanked his T-shirt over his head. As hard as he planned to work at forcing useless dreams from his mind, he had to get ready to stink.

By early evening, he'd made good on that pledge and was covered in enough sweat and grime to prove it. He'd refused to break for dinner, but even working through starvation had failed to keep his focus on the 7d nails and the half-inch-thick plywood sheathing instead of on the comings and goings in the church drive. His desperate hope that Charity would return humiliated him. Only weakness could make him need her so much.

"See you tomorrow," Rusty called to the crew as seven pairs of work boots stomped back to their trucks.

Thankfully, Rusty had left him alone today, probably knowing more than he should yet keeping his mouth shut. He hadn't even asked for details on the trip to Indiana.

Rick glanced at the church in time to see Reverend Bob and Andrew coming out the door. At first, he welcomed that normal distraction, but then the two ministers walked directly his way.

"Rick, could we have a moment with you?" Reverend Bob said once he stepped to the bottom of the ladder.

"About last night," Andrew added unnecessarily.

Backing down the steps, Rick faced the two men and the subject he would have preferred to drop.

Turning to Andrew, he wanted to know, "What took you so long? I expected you to interrogate me this afternoon as soon as I got here."

"Interrogate?" Andrew grinned. "I would have called it quizzing, but never *interrogating*."

Reverend Bob gestured toward the picnic table and then led the other two men there. "Yesterday was quite a day."

As Rick sat on the bench, his gaze fell on the building that had come to represent only pain to him. "You can say that again."

Andrew sat beside him, leaning forward and resting his elbows on the table. "Charity had to have been devastated after meeting her father."

"Have you talked to her?" Rick looked back and forth between the two men who weren't providing answers quickly enough for his taste. "Is she okay?"

But Reverend Bob only shook his head. "She never returned home this morning."

Panic and guilt entwined as Rick fought for clarity. He'd been an idiot to let her drive home so upset. He pushed up from the table. "We've got to find her."

Andrew clasped a hand over Rick's shoulder before he could stand. "She's fine, man." He paused until Rick sat again. "She's fine."

"Charity stayed at a hotel in Novi," Reverend Bob explained. "She phoned her mother a few hours ago to let her know she was okay. Charity said she would come later for some of her things."

Rick pushed away the flutter of jealousy to the recesses of his mind where it didn't make him seem so pitiful. At least she was all right. He couldn't let it matter that she hadn't called him to say so. "She just needs some time to absorb it all."

"The news had to have come as a terrible shock," Reverend Bob agreed. "I understand you were with her when she met her father."

Rick raised an eyebrow. "Did Mrs. Sims tell you all of this?" Funny, he couldn't picture Laura airing her dirty laundry to her ministers.

Reverend Bob shook his head. "Afraid not. Mr. Sims called first thing this morning and told me the whole story. He said he wants us to help his daughter."

"She's going to need it," Rick answered.

Andrew nodded. "And she's going to need you."

Rick looked back and forth between the two men. "What do you mean?"

"As I said, Joseph Sims told me the *whole* story," Reverend Bob said.

His tone seemed to indicate that the story might have included a certain building contractor who was in love with Sims's daughter. Jerking up from the table, Rick stepped away and paced. "He had no right...."

"Perhaps not, but he's worried about his child." Reverend Bob set his elbows on the table, resting his chin on folded hands. "He's a dad. Andrew and I are both fathers, too. We understand his need to protect her."

"It's pretty late for him to start worrying about her now," Rick answered, shaking his head. "He deserted her, and now he's vying for Father of the Year?"

Andrew stood and stepped into Rick's pacing path, forcing him to stop. "This situation is going to require a lot of healing and a lot of forgiveness. Charity will need a friend like you—"

"That's strange coming from you, *Reverend* Andrew." Rick emphasized that title and crossed his arms over his chest. "From what she told me, you put her down without a second thought."

Andrew only shook his head and smiled. "You know as well as I do we can't pick which person we fall in love with. I think the Father has a plan all along…before our hearts are ever involved."

"Why would *I* know that?" Rick held that same rigid posture though his insides shook.

"Because you love Charity. At least her father says you do. And if that's true, you'll need to help her figure out how to put her life back together."

The man never touched him, but Rick would have sworn he'd slugged him in the chest. "She doesn't want me or my help."

Andrew laid a hand on his shoulder. "She just needs time to regroup. She'll reach out when she's ready."

"Hope she'll reach out for the one she really needs," Rick said more to himself than the other men.

"You were right, Bob," Andrew said, nudging Rick with his elbow. "God always had a great plan for Charity. And Mr. McKinley, here, is part of that plan.''

Rick tightened his crossed arms to show he didn't appreciate their humor. ''So what now? Do you know where she is? Has she talked to her dad?''

''Relax.'' Reverend Bob gestured with his hands wide, indicating he found his impossible request simple. ''You'll hear from her soon. If you need something to do in the meantime, you can pray.''

With that, the minister stood and took a few steps toward the parking lot. Andrew rounded the table and followed him.

''Where are you going now?''

Glancing back over his shoulder, Andrew answered, ''We need to minister to one of our members. Laura.''

''Are you kidding?'' Fists clenched, Rick came from behind the table and marched to them. ''She caused this whole mess. It was her lies—her vanity— that made her daughter question her whole life. Shouldn't you minister to the one who really needs your help?''

Reverend Bob's smile was one of understanding. ''They both need our support and our prayers. Jesus said the well have no need for a physician. We minister to the sick in body and soul. If churches were filled with perfect Christians, then we'd be out of work in a matter of weeks.''

''God loves all of us no matter how unlovable we are,'' Andrew said.

Rick could only nod, conviction ripping the steam

from every retort in his thoughts. No one could have been more unlovable than he, and God had reached out to him, anyway. Yet, he still wondered if he could forgive Laura for hurting the woman he loved—or Charity for walking away from him. Empty feelings of abandonment long and successfully buried emerged from their graves, refusing to be covered up again. Was he strong enough to forgive Charity when she'd caused him so much pain?

As if Andrew recognized that his comment had reached its mark, he held out his hand, and Rick grasped it. Rick and Reverend Bob shook hands, and then the two ministers walked to Andrew's car.

"You'll let me know as soon as you hear anything from Charity, right?" Rick called after them.

Andrew waved back at him. "Sure thing, Rick. Should we tell her you asked after her?"

Rick shook his head, and the other man nodded his acknowledgement. No matter how much she'd hurt him, no matter how raw he felt that she'd rejected his help—and him—he still had to be certain she was safe. Only when he knew for sure she would be okay could he start trying to figure out how to live without her.

Chapter Seventeen

Charity pulled alongside the only remaining vehicle in the church lot just after eight o'clock. The orange color of early evening had bowed to the deep blues and purples of night, but work continued on the building site under harsh, artificial lighting.

Without having seen his truck, she would have known which man would still be there, pushing himself beyond physical limits to prove his worth. And quite possibly to work off anger over a rejection.

Her insides shook as she opened the car door, but she gathered her courage and climbed out anyway. Only seventeen hours had passed since they were in this same lot, but everything was different. She was different.

The corners of her lips turned up in a smile, but insecurities mounted again, their weight pulling the expression from her face. *A day late and a dollar short.* The old saying haunted her. Not even a day has passed, really, but she still wondered if the things she'd said this morning had made their tomorrows impossible.

Father, I'm listening. Please lead me where You want me to go. She almost begged for comfort over the loss she anticipated, but a new wave of misery rolled over her before she could form a petition. Could she survive a future without Rick? Though her stomach clenched with anguish, she steadied her shoulders and nodded her head. With God on her side, she could do anything.

"Charity, is that you?"

She startled at the sound of Rick's voice, which he followed across the parking lot. When only a few feet separated them, he stopped and jammed his hands into his pockets, scuffing the asphalt with one work boot.

"Are you all right?" he asked.

"I'm fine," she answered, with the assurance that one day soon God would make it so.

His anxiousness seemed to disappear, replaced by a confusing, thumbs-through-the-belt-loops aloofness. "I heard you stayed in Novi."

She wondered if it was bitterness she heard in his voice and tried to keep the hurt from hers. "Reverend Bob must have told you."

He nodded. "Did you see your mother?"

"I saw her. Talked to her. I'm staying at a hotel for a while. I'm probably not moving back home."

"Sorry to hear that," he said and cleared his throat.

"Reverend Bob and Andrew were at Mother's

when I went by. She needed them there. She was pretty upset.''

"Regret is a powerful emotion.''

How he could say something so profound—and so profoundly personal to her—without the slightest visible emotion, she didn't know. She couldn't hold her feelings at bay, not anymore, not when their future was at stake.

Twisting her hands together, she told him, "You're right. It is powerful.''

He shot a glance at her but quickly looked back to the brightly lit site. "We accomplished a lot today.''

How long would they continue discussing these inane things while the most important subjects remained off-limits? But she only said, "It looks like it. I bet you did most of the work.''

"Don't I smell like it?'' He paused as if waiting for laugh that didn't come. "We're going to have to burn the midnight oil to even have a chance of meeting the deadline. If even one subcontractor is late, we won't make it.''

"Can we stop this?'' Either the plea in her voice or the words themselves must have reached him because he turned back to her. "I want to talk to you. Really talk.''

"What's left to say?''

"Everything.'' Her voice broke then, but she refused to let her emotions rule her. On this, the saddest yet happiest day of her life, she would accept the answers she found now as God's will and walk forward into her future. She cleared her throat. "Something happened today."

Instead of answering, Rick stepped past her, opened the tailgate on his truck and sat down. He patted the metal next to him, and she sat beside him. Only inches separated them, but it seemed an unbridgeable gap. Maybe it had to be, and she would just have to accept it.

When the silence became so overpowering that she could no longer bear it, she finally said the words she'd yet to express aloud but that shouted in her soul. "Rick, I met God today…for the first time."

She expected questions from him, or at least a raised eyebrow. But he only turned and grasped her hand between both of his. "He's pretty great, isn't He?"

"Yes, He is. I never realized how different it could be if I only opened my heart to Him."

His bright smile faded as he looked down at their joined hands. Slowly, he released his grasp and pulled away. Clearing his throat, he scanned the various church buildings, not meeting her gaze. It was as if he knew he'd been found out—that his hardened exterior no longer masked his tender feelings inside—and he wanted to cover his lapse. Just as she'd pretended her heart hadn't been susceptible to his from the start.

"About this morning," she started out. The need to gather the words she'd spoken earlier and inhale them back into her lungs gripped her, but she wouldn't waste her time with futility. "Please forgive me."

"There's nothing to forgive." He continued to stare at some faraway place. "It's been a difficult day for you. You only said what you felt."

"Not everything I felt, Rick." She waited. No, she wouldn't speak to the side of his head. Let him answer whatever he would, but she planned to say it to his face.

When she would have given up, he finally turned to face her. And, like her, he waited.

"I love you. I think I have almost from the beginning, no matter how much I tried to ignore my heart's needs. And it…I…always needed you."

He opened his mouth to respond, but she couldn't let him. Not yet. She knew his history, how much he'd been hurt in the past. Even how much she must have hurt him by walking away after he'd admitted his feelings for her. He loved her. Only now, though many hours delayed, the truth of his admission fluttered over her, covering her with the temptation to hope. But would he be able to trust her enough to risk her hurting him again?

She touched an index finger to his lips to hush him. "This morning, after I learned that I'd based my life on lies, nothing seemed possible. Not even a future with you, no matter how much I wanted it. Now, only a few hours later, nothing seems *impossible*."

"A lot of difference a few hours make," he said, but he didn't sound convinced of that difference or of that promise for their future.

Charity pressed on. She needed him to understand what she was feeling. Her heart depended on it.

"No more lies, Rick. It doesn't even matter that I don't know myself all that well yet. I'm a work in progress, but I want to make that progress by your side."

Tasting the tears she'd promised herself she wouldn't cry, she grasped both his hands so tightly her fingers ached. "I want to live an honest life…with you."

"Well, why didn't you say so?" The question had barely escaped his lips before he leaned forward and covered her mouth with his. Theirs was a kiss of commitment. Of permanence.

"Do you think you can let go of my hands?" he whispered against her cheek. "They're going numb."

Charity opened her fingers but only wrapped her arms around his waist, reveling in the comfort of being enclosed in his arms. So sweet and perfect, she never wanted the moment to end as he placed gentle kisses on her cheeks, her eyelids, even her nose.

After only a few seconds, or minutes or hours passed, Rick pulled away, his hands still resting on her shoulders. "So where do we begin?"

"You could start by proposing to me."

With a salute, he hopped off the tailgate and leaned on one knee right on the asphalt. "Charity, I would like nothing better than to be your husband for the next ninety years. Please be my wife."

"Okay, but only for ninety years. Not a day longer."

"Deal." He lifted to seal the agreement with a kiss and sat beside her again. "Next?"

"I'll have to find someplace to live, at least until we get married."

"Any chance you'll move back in with your mother?" he said, brushing his fingers through her hair.

"I don't think so."

When he started to say something, she raised a hand to delay him. "I know I have to forgive my parents. God has, so I should, too. But I think healing is going to take some time. A lot of time."

"They don't deserve forgiveness," he grumbled.

"None of us do."

He shrugged. "Are you planning a long engagement?"

Charity grinned at that. "Not too long. Any time before December. That's my birthday."

"Oh, the dreaded thirty." He twisted a lock of her hair around his fingers. "Wouldn't want you to hit that milestone without a wedding ring."

"None of that matters anymore. I just can't wait to be your wife." She leaned over to him again, touching her lips to his once. Then again.

Clearing his throat, he held her away from him. "I agree. No long engagement." He coughed into his hand. "Let me get this building project finished. We can plan a wedding right after that."

"Sounds good to me. I have plenty to do in the meanwhile. I have a new walk with God to work on and some relationships with my parents to rebuild."

Rick chuckled and wrapped his arm around her shoulder. "I have some Sunday work to do, too. I've decided to get involved in the local church. I want to play an active role, on the facilities committee or something."

"Why the change?" She leaned into his shoulder, inhaling his scent of hard work and the outdoors.

"This really smart woman I know convinced me there's an imperfect group that has a perfect place for me." He leaned to kiss the top of her head.

"My mission from the start…accomplished." She didn't have to thank Rick for his own outreach mission. It was understood. "Oh, and I have one more important thing to do. I have a sister I need to get to know."

As Charity rested her head on his shoulder, they stared at the building that had first introduced them. Constructed in truth, they could now build a life together filled with hope and love.

"Promise me you won't forget about me during all of these big projects," Rick said, squeezing her shoulder.

"Not on your life," she said, smiling into the darkness. "All our lives."

On the Saturday before Thanksgiving, Charity stared into the mirror while Hannah tucked some stray hairs beneath the comb in the bride's fingertip veil. Wafts of fresh roasted turkeys and pumpkin pies caused Charity's stomach to growl loudly.

"Reception hunger is interrupting my wedding day jitters," she joked.

"My mouth is watering, too." Hannah inhaled deeply and backed away two steps to admire her handiwork. "You look beautiful, Charity. Perfect."

"Quit it or you'll make me nervous."

Hannah tilted her head and shrugged. "Sorry. But you just amaze me. I can't believe you've pulled this whole wedding together in—what—two months?"

"Ten and a half weeks to be exact." Charity bent and brushed at nonexistent wrinkles on the silk fabric and lace appliqués of her gown. "Compared to our courtship, our engagement has been an eternity."

Hannah chuckled as she leaned close to the mirror, lining her eyes with a gray pencil. "You can say that again. But I still don't know how you did it. Most of our church's brides take a whole year to plan a wedding. What's your secret?"

Charity straightened and grinned at the young woman she'd grown much closer to since the day when her life changed on so many levels. Perhaps the losses of their mothers—in very different ways—drew them together.

"You buy your gown off the rack. You order invitations and the cake immediately and pray every night that the reception facility will be completed by your wedding day."

"But there were so many details. You did so much so quickly," Hannah said as she put her cosmetics away and turned to face the bride again. Carefully, she lowered the veil's blusher over Charity's face.

"Tricia helped me a lot. It sure made it easier planning our wedding the day of the church Thanksgiving celebration and the Family Life Center dedication, so we'll have the best reception dinner ever. With the church's best cooks making the food, it's going to be awesome."

"You've got that right. Coordinating the events was pure genius. But you'd better hope Dad doesn't get too long-winded during the ceremony, or your guests will be sneaking out to snack."

"Reverend Bob promised he'd be brief, but there still might be a few slipping out for a turkey leg."

Someone knocked on the door of the women's rest room. "Ladies, are you about ready?" Andrew called from outside the door. "The guests are ready to revolt—or eat up the reception. They're all waiting in the gym."

Hannah checked Charity's makeup for the umpteenth time and straightened her own mauve maid-of-honor dress. "We'll be right out."

"Hurry," some unidentified voice called from outside. "The groom is as white as a sheet."

Both women laughed until Hannah turned Charity to face the mirror. Struck silent, she could only stare at her amazing one-hour transformation into bride. Emotion welled in her throat, but she choked it back.

"Thanks for all your help, Hannah. You're a gem."

"It was fun." Hannah fiddled with Charity's chapel-length train, unfastening the bustle loops.

"You do realize your train will be covered with concrete dust by the time you make it down the aisle."

"I know. Mother's already had a fit or two about it. She can't understand why I didn't want the ceremony in the church sanctuary." Charity shrugged. "She didn't get the symbolism of us being married in the new building."

"You know your mother. Not a big fan of breaking tradition. Laura probably wishes she could be in here helping you get ready instead of waiting outside with the other guests." Hannah's expression turned wistful, as if she was remembering her own mother who had never lived long enough to see her as a bride.

"I know, but healing takes time," Charity said, hugging her friend.

Hannah squeezed her one last time and opened the door. "This is going to be an event to remember."

But the hubbub in the hallway of church members carrying holiday dishes one direction and wedding gifts the other way made Charity question the wisdom of combining the three significant celebrations.

"Don't worry," Hannah said over her shoulder as she led Charity into the hallway. "It's just a little crazy because the wedding guests can't be seated until you cut the ribbon."

Rounding the corner, Charity approached Laura, who was dressed in a flattering navy silk dress. Tears filled Laura's eyes, and she dabbed at them with a handkerchief.

"Hello, Mother." She leaned close for a hug. "You look beautiful."

"No, you, sweetheart, are the beautiful one," Laura said, clasping her daughter's hands as they pulled away from each other. "What a lovely bride you make. You've picked a great groom, too."

Charity smiled at her mother, realizing how hard she was trying to make amends.

Prelude music filtered through the same crowded hallway from which Joseph emerged. Charity touched her mother's hand and then turned to hug her father.

"Honey, I'm so happy for you," Joseph said with another squeeze. "Julia was able to make it after all. She was so worried about finishing her midterm projects, but I don't think she'd miss this for the world."

Charity pulled back and smiled at him. "I can't wait to meet her face-to-face. I feel like I already know her from all the telephone calls."

Farther down the hallway, Tricia waited with the children, all scrubbed and in their Sunday best.

"You're so pretty, Miss Charity," Lani crooned. "You look like my wedding doll."

"She'll be Mrs. Charity now," Rusty Jr. corrected.

"I want to call her Aunt Charity to go with Uncle Rick. Is that okay?" Lani said, giving her brother a superior look.

Charity nodded, so close to tears she couldn't answer aloud. Making her way around the children, she hugged Tricia, grateful for her growing circle of friends.

"Excuse me, everyone," Reverend Bob said from the front of the crowd. "Who is ready for a wedding?"

A few whoops went up from the mass of bodies, and finally a path appeared down the center of the hallway.

And she saw him.

Standing next to his best man, Rusty, Rick didn't look like his regular tan self against the white tuxedo jacket. His skin appeared pasty. But then his gaze covered her from the floral ring in her hair to her gown's scalloped hem, giving her a case of nerves. His smile and wink, though, sent that anxiety floating away.

Father, thank you so much for leading me to Rick, Charity prayed without moving her lips as she stared at him. *Thank you for showing me he was one of Your promises for my life. Amen.*

"Could everyone please allow the bride past so we can get on with the ceremony?" Reverend Bob requested, and the path immediately widened.

Within a few seconds, Hannah and Charity had reached the front, where the two ministers stood with Rick and Rusty. Tessa appeared beside them in a mauve flower girl dress, her hair in a little girl updo. Charity smiled down at the curly-haired child who grinned back.

A huge red ribbon crossed the doorway into the fellowship hall portion of the building. Beyond it, folding chairs were lined in rows.

"Hello, my beautiful bride," Rick said in a quiet voice that could be heard by only those closest to them, but those few quickly relayed the quote to the rest of the crowd. He reached for Charity's hand and tucked it in the crook of his arm before turning back to the minister.

"This day is the result of many prayers," Reverend Bob began. "All of us at Hickory Ridge have waited a long time for this day of dedicating the Family Life Center. Though buildings don't make a church family, this does symbolize a new beginning for all of us." He indicated the walls that still smelled of fresh paint.

"How more perfect to combine this event with the celebration of the beginning of Rick and Charity's new life together as well as our annual event where we give thanks for God's many blessings."

"So let's do it. We're starved," called a youthful voice from the back of the crowd.

Reverend Bob chuckled. "On that note, let's cut the ribbon." He handed a pair of scissors to Andrew, another for Rick and Charity to share and kept one for himself. "On three. One...two...three." With a trio of snips, the ribbon fell into pieces on the ground.

"Let's have a wedding," someone called out. Already the crowd poured forward into the room, filling the chairs.

Rick and Charity waited until last and then, with joined hands, they took that first big step into the new building and into their future.

*   *   *   *   *

Dear Reader,

I really enjoyed revisiting the people of Hickory Ridge
Community Church in this story. These characters have
become so real for me, their ties to each other so
powerful, like those in the church of my childhood.
Though not perfect, they care for each other and
worship together.

Writing Charity Sims's story was a special joy because
Charity has so much to learn about life, matters of the
heart and, especially, God's love. Who better to teach
her than the reluctant hero, Rick McKinley? This story
is about living *An Honest Life* before others and in our
own hearts. Through God's love we can finally find
peace.

I love hearing from readers. You may write to me at
P.O. Box 120044, Grand Rapids, MI, 49512, or contact
me through the web site
http://www.loveinspiredauthors.com.

Dana Corbit